The Club

By D. Dwayne Edward

The Club

Published by Curiosity Press
United States of America

ISBN (Hardcover): 979-8-9943105-3-3
ISBN (Paperback): 979-8-9943105-4-0
ISBN (eBook): 979-8-9943105-5-7

Library of Congress Control Number: In Process

Author: D. Dwayne Edwards

First Edition

For my good friend, Todd, thank you for your support and encouragement.

Prologue

Colombia sits at the strategic crossroads of South America. To the north, the Antioquia Department has direct access to the Caribbean and, from there, to the Atlantic. Less than 200 kilometers west, across the neighboring Chocó region, lay the Pacific Ocean. Geography alone makes Antioquia a natural hub for commerce and for crime.

For half a century, cartels had operated there with ruthless efficiency. Pablo Escobar's Medellín cartel once ruled with near-sovereign authority, its legacy absorbed and adapted by smaller but no less dangerous groups. These bandas criminales, loosely organized but highly lethal, served as both enforcers and diversions. By keeping Colombian police tied down in constant low-level skirmishes, they provided the larger cartels with insulation. It was a layered defense system, cheap, expendable, and brutally effective.

The Colombian state fought back with limited resources. Combined, the police and military spent more than $100 million annually on drug interdiction, an immense sum for Bogotá, but a fraction of the problem. Washington knew it. For the United States, cocaine was not just a narcotics issue, but a national security threat. The DEA alone maintained a $500 million annual budget dedicated to Colombian operations. The other three-letter agencies, the CIA, NSA, and FBI, were deeply invested in the matter. The combined American effort is estimated to be in the billions of dollars.

Still, the numbers favored the cartels. United Nations analysts estimated the global narcotics economy at more than $40 billion each year. Colombia controlled a third of that, producing nearly seventy percent of the world's cocaine. Almost every gram destined for the United States passed through its mountains, rivers, or ports.

The logistics were formidable and brilliant. The Panama Canal, a century-old artery of global commerce, saw forty ships pass through it each day between the Atlantic and Pacific. For the cartels, it was opportunity incarnate. In a sea of legitimate traffic, their shipments moved like ghosts. Drugs outbound, cash inbound. By conservative projections, Colombian cartels would generate $25 billion annually by 2030; untaxed, unregulated, unstoppable.

Production, transportation, and distribution were the machine's visible parts. The real challenge lay elsewhere. For all their ruthlessness, the cartel leaders faced many of the same problems as any Fortune 500 CEO: liquidity. Traditional corporations sought ways to maximize profits without increasing the tax burden on those profits.

The cartels' ongoing challenge was to transform the illicit billions into clean, honest, and usable assets.

Money laundering wasn't just a side business. It was the business. And in that shadow war of numbers, banks, and offshore accounts, the cartels played as ruthlessly as they did in the jungles of Antioquia.

In rooms filled wall-to-wall with hundred-dollar bills, there was a legacy of crimson blood on each one of those green pieces of linen sporting the face of an American inventor and patriot. In its quest to wash all that cash, there would be much more blood spilled.

What the cartel needed was a completely new model for the laundry business. And a small port city on a river that defined the boundary between two Pacific Northwest states looked to have just what they needed.

Hole #1 – "Sidewinder" 437-yard Par 4

At 06:57 AM, Taylor Duncan nosed his grandfather's golf cart off the asphalt path, its worn rubber tires thumping as they passed over a drainage grate. He brought it to a stop near the blue tee markers on the par-four first hole. The small two-stroke gas engine ticked lazily, coughing faint puffs of exhaust into the crisp morning air.

Duncan was twenty-four, half an inch under six feet, and built like an athlete who never missed workouts. His stride had a rhythm, the unconscious cadence of someone who once marched to drill sergeants' commands or had watched enough movies to pick up the style.

He had striking features: short blond hair, a jaw sharp enough to cut glass, and pale blue eyes that focused intensely, whether on fairways or women.

Duncan has been playing at the Columbia Valley Golf & Country Club since he was eight. His father's membership opened the gates, but the bylaws were clear: at twenty-three, you paid your own way. Taylor was now a Junior Member, dues deducted monthly like clockwork. He didn't mind the bill; he liked the perks: a pool in summer, a sauna in winter, and a clubhouse where bourbon was cheaper than anywhere downtown.

This morning, he pushed the envelope in another way. He broke Club rules, and rules were rules.

First, he went on the course without notifying the Pro Shop; and secondly, he used another member's golf cart. Papa Dave's cart usually sat idle in the garage, as the seventy-seven-year-old only played once a week. To Taylor, that was an opportunity. He borrowed it without explicitly asking.

He locked the brake, stepped out, and followed his routine. He slid a glove onto his left hand, grabbed a sleeve of Pro V1s from his bag pocket, and tossed the driver head cover into the basket behind the seat. He grabbed a tee and checked his pocket for the half joint he planned to light up once he was far from the clubhouse and curious eyes.

He approached the tee box like a man entering a familiar battlespace.

Sixteen years on this course had made every contour, gully, and bunker part of his mental map. He knew where a drive needed to land, where it shouldn't, and how to force opponents into mistakes. In competition, he always had the range advantage, outdriving members, visitors, and even his own father. The real edge, however, came on the greens. He could sink twenty-five-footers with remarkable consistency.

He placed a ball on the tee, stepped back, and loosened his shoulders. His Ping G430 Max gleamed in the early light, made from 7075 aerospace-grade aluminum in the shaft, featuring a carbon-fiber crown and a face milled with machine-precision grooves designed to reduce spin rates, a weapon disguised as sports equipment.

Taylor swung twice, loosening muscles still fogged from the three bourbons he had with Stacie Broomer the night before. He smiled at the thought; country clubs were half social theater, half minefield, but quickly refocused. He addressed the ball, shifted his weight, exhaled, and drove down through the swing.

The explosion came first.

A deep, concussive "BOOM" rolled across the fairways, not the sharp bark of a small engine misfiring but something heavier and lower. His shot went wild, slicing left and vanishing into a stand of century-old blackjack pines two hundred yards down the fairway.

"Son of a bitch." His temper flared, and he raised his club to pound the ground, then stopped, remembering the $500 price tag on the driver in his hand. He looked around the grounds: no crew, no equipment in sight.

He shoved the club back into his bag and pushed the cart forward, following the line of his errant shot. At the treeline, he spotted two figures on the nearby fairway: one he thought might be a new groundskeeper, the other unmistakably Davis Pearson, the Course Superintendent and a fixture on the course since before Taylor was born.

Within minutes, Pearson pulled up in his work truck, still rocking the mullet he'd worn three decades ago, though time had thinned it. "Yo, Taylor, what's going on?"

"Morning, Davis. One of your rigs backfired over there?" Taylor pointed.

"Something like that," Pearson said, face neutral. "Equipment's old, the course is old. Pipes older. Half my time's fixing leaks. Water's expensive."

Nothing that had just come out of Pearson's mouth had registered with Taylor as he crouched by his ball, nodding. "Looks like that backfire cost me par."

"Didn't think anyone would be out before eight, nothing was on the book," Davis replied. His eyes flicked briefly toward the trees.

Taylor felt the sting. It was necessary to check in at the pro shop before teeing off. He hadn't. He was also riding in Papa Dave's cart. Breaking one rule was manageable; breaking two was dangerous. Davis could report him, and the Board might hand down fines or worse.

Taylor quickly stood and adopted the look of an apologetic yet spoiled child. He needed to fix this. "I'm sorry, Davis. I was out late with Stacie Broomer, maybe had one more drink than I should have, and forgot to update the tee sheet online. My bad. It won't happen again."

Pearson gave a short nod, looked at the golf ball buried in a tangle of pine needles and small branches, then turned his truck back toward the trees. "Good luck with that shot."

Taylor retrieved a six iron, now concentrating solely on salvaging a bogey. He never noticed the way

Pearson parked again beside the second work truck, or how the 'groundskeeper' named Pedro leaned against it, spitting tobacco into the grass. He never overheard their brief conversation.

"What the fuck did that little puto want?" Pedro growled.

"Lost a ball when the... " Davis raised two fingers in mock air quotes, "'truck backfired.'"

Both men looked down at the four-foot-deep hole by their feet. The man inside was likely in his fifties, dressed in an Italian suit of expensive wool, with an Armani tie askew. A clean 9mm entry wound centered on his forehead. Blood darkened and pooled against the dirt.

Pedro laughed as he kicked the corpse into the freshly dug hole. "Damn, dude, killed by a backfire. Hell of a hazard on this course."

***

A hundred and fifty yards away on the green of hole number one, Taylor missed his par putt by three inches. His curse at the sky echoed across the empty fairway, masking the quieter sound of dirt hitting a body.

He strode to the cart, vigorously marked a five on the scorecard, and shifted into forward. The cart hesitated, then shot off toward the next tee box, about thirty yards away.

What made him an excellent golfer, beyond his physical skills, was his focus and his ability to reset his energy. He never replayed the last hole. His attention was on preparing for the next.

Before walking up to the next box, he ran through his regular rituals. Then, he added another temporary ritual by lighting that joint. He planned to make up that bogey on this hole.

Hole #2 – "Columbia View" 404-yard Par 4

On paper, Mariana Pearson was a fifth and sixth-grade Spanish teacher in the small town of Kalama, twelve miles south of Columbia City. To parents, she was patient, structured, and kind. To Davis Pearson, the Superintendent, she was his new bride.

Before she became Mrs. Pearson, she was Mariana González López. That name carried weight. Her bloodline linked her directly to Jhon Jairo González, the patriarch of Colombia's largest narcotics cartel in Antioquia Department.

From the outside, their marriage seemed like pure luck. But in reality, fate played no role in it.

***

[Intercept // NSA Fort Meade // 2023-11-14   03:17:26Z]

Query Flagged: "dating apps, Kalama, Washington"

Traffic Pattern Analysis: Increased outbound metadata from device tagged *Mariana G.* Encrypted

WhatsApp calls trace to Medellín ISP. Probability of narco-affiliate infiltration: 72%.

***

Mariana deliberately gamed the system. On her dating apps, she filtered for men in influential roles, such as trucking and logistics, cruise line managers, boutique financial advisors, and gatekeepers of exclusive clubs like yacht clubs and golf courses.

These men naturally acted as nodes within networks of movement, money, and influence.

Davis was one of the few she swiped right on. Middle management. An open book. A man who vented about members' tantrums over tee times and irrigation systems. A man who answered her innocent questions, "How many members? Do they all pay? How much?" with detail. Data points, really, each one feeding into her expanding map of the Columbia River corridor, the numerous ports, and the choke points between the Pacific and Portland.

She played her part well. Her English was excellent, having been refined at a British Virgin Islands boarding school, but with Davis, she pretended to have gaps.

Every time Davis clarified, each story about logistics or finances gave her more understanding. The woman asked about dues and amenities. The operative recorded infrastructure and revenue streams.

And still, she hadn't expected to fall in love.

That had been the variable, the bonus.

***

A week after Davis announced his plans during her visit to Columbia City, Mariana headed south. She passed Medellín's concrete sprawl, crossed jungle ridgelines, and entered her uncle's guarded compound.

The González residence didn't look like a fortress or a flashy palace. Still, its security was on par with any billionaire's, layered: biometric scanners at the inner perimeter, encrypted radios clipped to the belts of men wearing trucker caps and carrying sub-machine pistols hidden under windbreakers with logos for Red Bull and Dos Hombres Mezcal.

They found it funny and a bit ironic to be wearing the brand of two actors who starred in a very famous TV series about making drugs.

Mariana looked up to see a drone lazily circling overhead. The disguise of simplicity was, in itself, a tactic.

Jhon Jairo González sat poolside, his linen shirt unbuttoned, revealing his tanned, prominent stomach as he watched his grandchildren cannonball into the water. He smiled with the joy of a proud, aging patriarch. His laugh echoed across the veranda, and the children in the pool joined in his mirth. However, this man built his empire not on happiness but on drugs and the bodies of those who opposed him. His nickname was 'el garrote' for the nine-iron he often used to beat his victims to death.

When Mariana entered the patio, her daughters, twelve-year-old Isabella and fourteen-year-old Gabriela, ran into their great-uncle's arms. He hugged them warmly, embodying a family scene.

As they pulled away and hurried toward the pool's edge, his eyes shifted to Mariana; they sharpened like a banker reviewing balance sheets.

"Mariana," he said, his baritone voice filling the air, "it has been too long." After a polite hug and kiss on his cheek, he handed her a glass of iced tea. The weight of expectation was as clear as the ice clinking in the glass.

***

[Overhead Imagery // KH-12 Recon Satellite // Lat: 6.255N Long: 75.582W //

Medellín   AO]

SIGINT correlation: thermal signatures, 24 pax.

Notable object: metallic case, 1m length, heat-dense, carried into veranda 14:32 local.

Assessment: probable weapons shipment or a secure financial ledger case.

***

Politics, religion, and money were the three pillars of Jhon's power. Politicians could be helpful when you padded their re-election coffers. And although he attended church regularly, per his mother's dying wish, Jhon Jairo did not honestly believe in God. He went through the motions of sacraments out of habit, not faith. His real religion was money.

In his world, and through his eyes, money performed daily miracles.

***

A Ugandan farmer sustains his family for another month with a 20,000 Ugandan shilling note. Miracle. A Russian oligarch buys his son a $3 million racing yacht. Miracle. A Boston kid finds a $20 bill and treats his friends to ice cream. Miracle. And in Bienville Parish, Louisiana, a hemp farmer pays off his loan in cash. Miracle.

By those standards, Jhon Jairo was a saint. His empire generated $10 billion in annual revenue, with profit margins above 67%. Higher than Apple, cleaner than Tesla, and free from shareholder interference. His ledger was simple: family and loyalty. Respect the patriarch and serve the machine, and you succeed. Failing at either, and somebody could erase you.

***

[CIA / CTC SOUTHCOM Division / Situation Report   Extract]

Target: GONZÁLEZ,   Jhon   Jairo

Estimated   Revenue: $6.0B   /   annum

Profit   Margin: 67%

Operational   Note: Family   integration   = resilience.   Bloodline   loyalty   makes   infiltration difficult. Recommended: target out-marriages, e.g., niece Mariana (*US asset of opportunity*).

***

Mariana understood the risks. Family ties could either open doors or pose deadly threats. Still, she also knew her uncle appreciated creativity. He valued innovations in logistics, finance, or smuggling just as much as he valued ruthlessness.

As she sipped sweet iced tea beside him, her daughters laughing in the background, she prepared to present her idea.

A country club in the Pacific Northwest. Membership lists are packed with shipping executives, bankers, and investors. Secure grounds, covert movements, cash flows disguised as dues and bar tabs. A staging ground not for golf, but for empire.

Her uncle leaned forward, eyes narrowing in amusement. "Tell me, Mari," he said. "What is the new miracle you bring me today?"

Hole #3 – "Holey Grail" 487-yard Par 5

Religion has always been a double-edged sword. It offers comfort, but also causes harm. It justifies wars and peace treaties, crusades and charities. Faith provides structure, purpose, and hope, yet it can also serve as an excuse for bloodshed.

Golf is no different.

The golfers of Columbia View carried themselves with the same quiet confidence as parishioners in a cathedral. Paid staff helped Club members find that "God-given" talent, reinforcing it through ritual: endless hours at the driving range, precision putts on the practice green, and the sacrificial spending of money on each new club or swing analyzer, promising absolution from bogey.

Rituals create a sense of belonging. Rituals establish hierarchy. And hierarchy fosters exclusivity.

***

[Treasury Dept // FinCEN Suspicious Activity Report // Case ID 22-5791]

Subject: "Private Membership Clubs / Pacific Northwest"

Flagged Transaction: $175,000 initiation fee wired via offshore trust, Grand Cayman → Oregon.

Assessment: Possible laundering pathway.

Pattern matches prior narco-front infiltration attempts.

***

The U.S. golf industry made over $100 billion in 2024. Country clubs alone were worth tens of billions of dollars. That amount of money drew scrutiny. It also served as a perfect cover.

Exclusivity was deliberate, not accidental. Clubs managed access with initiation fees and dues ranging from 5% to 10% of an applicant's gross yearly income. Money represented loyalty. Financial stability was like a baptism. Contributions were made through patronage. Everyone who proved their worth was welcomed into the group.

Discrimination based on race and religion has diminished over time. In theory, it had disappeared, but in practice, it merely changed its form. Green remained the only color that truly mattered.

***

[CIA Directorate of Analysis // Cultural Intelligence   Note]

Subject: "Golf Clubs as Cultural Gateways"

Observation: Membership functions as soft power access to finance, shipping, and local politics.

Actionable Insight: Boards of Directors serve as gatekeepers. Vetting mirrors counterintelligence review, but with no legal oversight. Vulnerable to manipulation by external influence ops.

***

Board meetings resembled councils of elders. Membership applications were presented, examined, and voted on.

Approval required a majority consent, with each raised hand as binding as a clerical blessing. Behind closed doors, they decided who would kneel at the altar of exclusivity and who would be excommunicated.

In that sense, country clubs were cathedrals of capitalism, with their members worshipping not at stained-glass windows but on manicured greens. Their commandments were inscribed not in scripture but in balance sheets. Their ministers carried wedges instead of incense.

And for operatives like Mariana González López, these places weren't just playgrounds for the wealthy. They were nodes. Access points. Opportunities.

***

[SIGINT Intercept // NSA-OREGON FIELD NODE // 2023-11-21 19:04:56Z]

Audio Capture, Columbia View CC Boardroom:

"...applicant owns three logistics depots in Tacoma, claims annual revenue of $45M..."

[Transcript redacted: 00:32:14 – 00:37:58]

End Note: Coded language suggests tacit discrimination. Financial probity remains the primary filter.

***

Ultimately, the game was never only about golf. It was about trust, status, and money.

Hole #4 – "Uplands Meadow" 325-yard Par 4

Davis Pearson and the man the crew knew only as Pedro worked quickly. The body was already in the trench; no one else had come across their work.

They tamped down the soil in thin layers, replaced the sod, and swept sand into the seams until the cut lines disappeared. If you didn't know where to look, you wouldn't notice it. They knew. That was the point. They knew where the bodies were buried.

It had been too close with Taylor Duncan. A 150-acre course within Columbia's city limits meant members could appear anywhere, anytime. In the 1920s, this land was farmland and river fog; now it's lined with cul-de-sacs, contractors, and HOA boards.

The river still curves west toward the Pacific fifty miles further downstream, splitting Oregon from Washington like a steel ruler. The city's founders had sold livability; the current council manages liability.

Before standing, Pearson ran a gloved thumb along the last seam and nodded once. Pedro didn't nod; he just scanned the trees and listened. In the distance, he could hear Taylor's cart chugging its way to the next tee box. Pedro would watch that one. Something about these Club members rubbed him the wrong way; they all had a sense of invulnerability and entitlement.

Pedro didn't care for these people generally, and now his focus would be on Taylor Duncan.

If Taylor knew this, if he realized that a man who had bragged about how many bodies he had buried over the past ten years was now watching him, Taylor would've freaked out.

***

[USG // DHS I&A NOTE // 2025-03-11 14:42Z]

Subject: *Municipal Work Orders – Columbia City,*   *OR*

Finding: Unlogged excavation near Columbia View G&CC, Hole #1/#4 junction.

Data Source: Smart-meter voltage dip + irrigation controller event (Toro Lynx, FW 5.4.2).

Action: Notify FBI Portland RA if a second anomaly occurs within 30 days.

***

Special Agent Patrick "Pat" Garrot sank into one of two barrel-back leather chairs in his office, which also served as his living room. He set a steaming mug of dark-roast coffee on a coaster shaped like a driver's head and looked out the picture window. The home where he currently lives was built in the 1930s by the town's first doctor.

From the outset, Dr. Roche operated his medical practice on the main floor, where Pat now sits, drinking from his mug. The second floor houses a fully equipped two-bedroom apartment where the doctor lived as he continued to grow and develop his practice.

After retirement, he reclaimed the main floor as his home. The exam rooms became bedrooms, the waiting room is now the living room, and the surgery became his kitchen. The upstairs was converted into a free museum showcasing everything train-related. At the turn of the 20th century, trains were a significant part of Kalama.

The Bureau purchased the house in 2015 to serve as an operational office and occasional safe house. When it wasn't assigned to a case, it was used as an Airbnb, allowing neighbors to become comfortable with the frequent comings and goings.

Three blocks west, I-5 runs between Portland and Seattle; farther out, twin rail lines parallel the interstate, feeding grain terminals along the riverbank. Beyond that, the Columbia River was a dull sheet of pewter under low clouds.

This town watched the traffic that moved people and money, just as arteries move blood. Trucks. Trains. Towboats. Past him, through him, around him, twenty-four hours a day. The rhythm was a metronome that let him think.

At times like this, Pat let his eyes de-focus and used the motion as a filter, like visual white noise. Box trucks alongside forty-footers; private cars with state plates from California to Vancouver, BC; the occasional oversize load with a pilot car and a prayer.

Pat watched the flow until a problem surfaced and snapped into focus. Today felt like a big-problem day.

At forty-five, Pat stayed fit because the job demanded it, and he felt centered when he was physically healthy. Chapel Hill had shaped him; the UNC golf team, a top-ten amateur, had a decent shot at a tour card if life had gone differently. Then the Bureau called, and he answered. Two decades later, he was still on the line.

Hazel Mae, fifty pounds of golden Lab and Rhodesian Ridgeback optimism, bounded into the room and onto a green mohair sofa, planted paws on the windowsill, and barked twice at the world.

Walk time. Pat drained his now lukewarm coffee, stood up, and headed for the back door.

"Stay or go?" he asked. Hazel didn't do nuance; she beat him to the mudroom by three strides. He laughed, grabbed her leash from the hook near the back door, and they stepped into a light rain.

The drive to their favorite lake took less than five minutes, but the dog moaned and squirmed as if it had been in the truck for hours.

Currently, Hazel was the only girl in Pat's life. It was difficult for him to pursue a serious relationship because his job required frequent relocation. Pat didn't do one-night stands. He was lonely, but not yet so lonely.

He parked his red Toyota pickup in the dirt lot on the east side of the lake, got out, and walked to the passenger door while sliding his holster to his side. He barely opened the door when Hazel burst out and started running toward the trail that circled the spring-fed lake.

It was stocked with a variety of Pacific NW species, making it a favorite spot for locals to spend an hour or so fishing before or after work. It was usually a pretty busy place. Today, a late-model sedan was the only car parked at the other end of the lot. Rain had kept the regulars away this morning.

Whoever was inside that other car was probably smoking or checking texts and emails.

As was his habit after years with the bureau, he noted the car's specifics. White, Chevy or GM sedan, lightly tinted windows, and a single occupant in the front passenger's seat. That was different.

From his position, he couldn't read the license plate. If the vehicle were still there when he finished their walk, he would have noted it as well. He rarely wrote anything down before working on case reports because he had an eidetic memory. He remembered everything as if he were viewing a photograph or a painting.

"Come on, Hazel, you take the lead." He pointed toward the trailhead, and she was off like a rocket. He chuckled as he picked up the pace to follow her.

They had barely gone halfway around the lake when his 'work phone' buzzed. He pulled it out of his pocket and checked the incoming number. Columbia City Country Club.

"Pat Garrot", he answered.

Good morning, Pat. This is Tom Douglas, general manager of the Columbia City County Club.

"Good morning, Mr. Douglas. I'm pleased to hear from you. I trust my references were worth the money I paid for them," then quickly, "joking."

Chuckling, he replied, "Please call me Tom, and yes, they were all glowing reviews. You, Pat, have a fan club.

***

[FBI // SIOC TELETYPE // PORTLAND RA]

Case: Cascadia/Whitecap   (Narco-Finance/Laundering)

SA: Patrick   GARROT   (ID-P4672)

Note: Assign temporary authority to exploit *non-custodial* municipal data feeds (traffic, utilities). Legal: NSL 18 USC §2709 (minimization in effect).

***

In Washington, D.C., Henry J. Wellborne III oversaw Science & Technology as the FBI's Executive Assistant Director. Publicly, he was known as "Mr. Wellborne" or "Director." Privately, with Tina, his wife, and precisely one agent he had mentored for years, he preferred to be called "Hank."

UNCC, Class of '83. Golf team member. He still checked college invitational leaderboards whenever he could steal time, which is how he first noticed a UNC player named Garrot at the 1996 NCAA regionals. The word had spread quickly: a second shot on a par-four that shouldn't have been possible, yet was.

He'd jogged hole to hole to catch up. The story, recorded in memory and a dozen poor photos: Garrot's towering drive following a perfect fade along a right-swept fairway; a crow erupting from a Douglas fir at the peak; the ball hitting the bird like a missile punching through a cockpit canopy. Feathers floated down. The ball dropped, dead stick, then bounced off roots and sat on what remained of the bird's head.

Rules official: play it as it lies or take a stroke. Garrot chose violence.

Three-wood. Two tempo swings. A stinger that soared twenty-five feet off the ground, skipping forward like a flat stone, kissed the front fringe and trundled to six inches. Birdie. The gallery, more than you'd expect for a regional, lost its collective mind. From that day, some joker called him "the Sheriff," as in Pat Garrett. The dead crow became "Billy the Corvid." College golf had its own gallows humor.

Wellborne introduced himself at the turn. They talked. They kept talking; email when email was new, coffee when calendars aligned: game theory, probability, sports psychology, the engineering of risk. Hank made reading lists; Pat consumed them.

Over a decade of Bureau work, Hank watched Pat solve problems like an economist with a badge.

When Wellborne established a new money-laundering task force, the first name on the list was Garrot.

***

[FBI // STB (Science & Tech Branch) // PROGRAM   BRIEF]

Unit: ARKSTONE   (Anti-Racketeering Knowledge   Systems)

Mission: Identify and neutralize laundering architectures supporting Colombian Drug trafficking organizations   (DTOs)   in   U.S.   jurisdictions.

Core Stack: Graph analytics (Neo4j w/ Bureau fork), Entity resolution (Senzing), Bank CTR/SAR fusion (FinCEN API), Maritime AIS anomaly detection (Unclosed Ocean 2.3), Club/Association Open-Source Extractor (CASE), Utility smart-grid side-channel flags (CobaltMains). Recruit: SA Patrick GARROT. Rationale: risk calculus + field instincts.

**

Seven years earlier, Garrot briefed the SIOC conference room on a pattern no one wanted to see: Colombian nationals with proven DTO links relocating near U.S. deepwater ports. Not Miami. Not L.A., newer, quieter locations like Tacoma, Portland, Savannah, and Toledo.

The pattern wasn't product; it was finance. They weren't moving kilos; they were moving credibility.

The Bureau's map flickered with private clubs and member lists, micro-economies with gated access and steady cash flows. Initiation fees served as onboarding costs. Dues acted as recurring charges. Events created surge capacity. Clubs represented culture; the ledgers resembled wash cycles.

Back on the Columbia View course, the history still showed in the bones. An old farmhouse had accreted into a clubhouse, one remodel at a time, with a granite foundation, eight thousand added square feet, the original root cellar and basement intact and rumored to be haunted.

Staff called it "the dungeon," and more than a few refused to go down there alone at closing time.

None of that changed the math. Courses leaked cash. Fairways required diesel, seed, chemicals, and steel: mowers, sprayers, topdressers; all capital-intensive. As a 501(c)(7), the Club belonged to its members and was run by an eight-person board. The bylaws allowed $150,000 in discretionary spending with a simple majority of the board; any expenditure over this amount needed a full-membership vote.

On paper, they had a couple of hundred members and collected $880,000 in dues annually.

Capacity projections claimed 450 members would generate $2.2 million, but growth had stalled at three to five new members each month, with attrition not far behind. The place was just treading water while posing for pictures.

That was before new money arrived. Quietly. Clean on the surface, chemically aggressive underneath.

***

[U.S. Treasury // FinCEN SAR EXTRACT // 2025-01-28]

Institution: Columbia River Community Bank (CRCB)

Pattern: Multiple initiation fees ($75k–$210k) routed via nested LLCs with beneficial owners masked behind BVI trusts; follow-on bar/banquet spends paid with sequential debit cards originating from the same prepaid issuer. Risk Score: 0.89 (High). Referral: FBI PORTLAND RA / ARKSTONE.

***

[NOAA // PORT AIS FEED // 2025-02-03]

Alert: Two bulk carriers (Panama-flag) delayed upriver by 18 hrs; pilotage variance request filed.

ARKSTONE Cross-Note: Variance window overlays with CRCB cash vault overfills (+22%) and Columbia View banquet revenue spikes (+240%). Assessment: Linked surge-wash event.

***

In the 1920s, golf sold the dream of leisure to industrialists. A century later, it sold something else: legitimacy. Membership boards gathered in quiet rooms and voted by majority. Who entered the cathedral of the green was never left to chance. It was controlled.

Within six months of targeting, cartel money, Mariana's money, was flowing through the Club. It started small, then grew larger. The culture shifted along with the ledger. New members with perfect references and aggressive tabs joined. Renovation proposals approached the $150,000 limit: irrigation controllers, bunker sand, and kitchen upgrades. Nothing flashy, just what was needed. That was the strategy: hide in plain sight.

On a gray morning that smelled like wet cedar and diesel, Davis Pearson and Pedro finished erasing a man from a fairway and turned their trucks toward the maintenance barn. Somewhere southeast along the interstate, a dog tugged a federal agent into the rain, and a graph database added a new edge to a growing, ugly picture.

***

[NSA // OREGON FIELD NODE // 2025-03-19   07:01:12Z]

Low-frequency acoustic anomaly captured near Columbia View G&CC (36 ms overpressure; profile = suppressed 9mm discharge or backfire from small   engine).

Correlated Events: Irrigation controller reboot (Hole #1 cluster), Two-device Bluetooth pairing (Cushman VIN redacted), Cellular handset (IMEI redacted) ephemeral on/off near pro shop (79 sec dwell).

Dissemination: FVEY // REL TO FBI. Minimization applied.

***

[FBI // ARKSTONE CASE LOG // 2025-03-19   15:42Z]

Analyst Note: Club accounts show linear revenue growth with non-linear spikes tied to member-only events. Vendor audit reveals shell-vendor overlap w/ Tacoma logistics firm (under review).

Field Action: SA Garrot to initiate *overtly benign* contact at Columbia View (pretext: junior member outreach/charity tournament). Parallel: subpoena CRCB account docs.

***

The Club's fairways remained the same width they'd always been. The angles still rewarded courage and punished arrogance. But the ground beneath the grass had changed. Money and blood had seeped into the soil. Once it did, it didn't wash out easily.

Hole #5 – "Miss Opportunity" 307-yard Par 4

For Pacific Northwesterners, June through September offered a welcome break. Warm days, cool nights, and just enough rain to keep every hill, valley, and cedar-shaded trail looking vibrant. Families filled trails and beaches; boaters tied up at docks with Yeti coolers, Bluetooth speakers, and more Tito's vodka and White Claws than sunscreen.

Golfers, though, were different. They weren't just outside; they were engaging in a form of worship.

The game entices because it's maddeningly simple on paper: four hits or fewer to sink a ball into a four-and-a-quarter-inch hole. Execution requires devotion, muscle memory, self-critique, and the almost-ritualistic upgrading of gear.

Loyal players invest in Titleist, Callaway, and Ping. Sacraments include $500 drivers and $300 shoes.

Golf occupied thoughts. The previous shot haunted. The next shot seemed inevitable. Sometimes, a hole from three weeks ago still echoed during dinner. Golf was a way of life.

***

[FBI // ARKSTONE Analyst Note // 2025-04-02]

Subject: U.S. Golf Economy – Vulnerability Scan. PGA Membership: ~27,000, Courses nationwide: 15,000+, Annual economic impact: $100B+

Observation: High density of nonprofit (501(c)(7)) structures = underregulated laundering conduits. Flag: "Prestige Initiation" model, fees >$150k in metro clubs, prime wash vector.

***

On a course, the rules were unforgiving. Par-three at 218 yards? You had one shot to prove your devotion. A clean strike from the tee, land softly, and read the green. The sand and trees stood like angels with flaming swords, guarding paradise. Miss, and penance ensued.

From a thousand feet above, drone, helicopter, balloon, the course looked like a circuit of meticulously groomed parks and hardscape arranged like jewelry: ponds reflecting the sky.

There were fountains hiding irrigation systems, bunkers as pale as Caribbean beaches. From above, the fairways appeared open, but every player knew the truth: the trees were sentinels positioned on the perimeter, forcing choices. Every line carried consequences.

Golf required patience. It also required money. Even the cheapest private clubs charged $5,000 a year, plus an initiation fee. The bigger names in major cities demanded six figures just to get in. And once you were inside? Dues, food minimums, assessments. Exclusivity was the goal. Pay to play is the norm.

***

[CIA // SOVAS (Social Venue Access Study) Extract]

Target Environment: Country Clubs / Golf Courses. Entry barrier: financial (initiation fees + dues). Gatekeeping: board vote, informal vetting, cultural bias → easily co-opted by DTO investment. Assessment: Ideal for embedding laundering operations; visible success aligns with cultural norms of "elite" membership.

***

On the ground, golf's sounds weren't hymns but small planes overhead, lawn mowers a few fairways away, curses carried by the breeze. Sound softened by trees still conveyed meaning.

A shout could signal triumph or fury; equipment rumbling might be machinery or cover noise.

Someone was always digging: irrigation leaks, drainage repairs, trench lines. A man with a shovel went unnoticed here. Dig a hole, fill it in. Dig another, fill it in. The rhythm of maintenance.

But in the shadows of hole five, that rhythm blurred the line between landscaping and cover-up. Holes weren't just for pipes. Sometimes, they were for people.

***

[NSA Field Node // OREGON Collection // 2025-04-05   13:17:22Z]

Sensor Sweep: Acoustic anomalies x3 within Columbia View G&CC perimeter (lat/long attached).

Pattern: 74 Hz ground compaction resonance consistent with tamped fill over disturbed soil.

Cross-Note: Matches prior DTO concealment tactics in Antioquia AO (Medellín 2019, Envigado 2021).

Dissemination: REL TO FBI / DEA.

***

Par-threes seemed brief on the scorecard. In reality, they were traps: one shot to clear the water, one chance to stay on the green, and one opportunity to avoid missing the hole.

And sometimes, when the fairways were under repair, revealing new turf lines after irrigation crews with muddy boots and gloves had been through, missing wasn't just about golf.

Hole #6 – "Cardiac Hill" 130-yard Par 3

Casey Brookfield set his ball on the tee, stepped back, and grabbed a nine-iron. At forty-seven, his swing was smooth enough to make younger players envious. The hit sounded solid and resonant, almost like a muted gong. The ball flew into the air, following a perfect arc toward the green, which was perched seventy-five feet above him.

Casey smiled, pleased with the shot. He'd named his GPS-enabled cart R2D2, and the machine dutifully followed the fob in his pocket as he walked uphill. His grin wasn't just for the shot; it was for the Board meeting tonight.

The numbers looked good. After years of stagnation, Columbia View Golf & Country Club was thriving. They added twenty-seven new members last month, bringing the total to nearly ninety so far this year. Initiation fees increased from $250 to

$5,000 without affecting demand. Since spring, almost half a million dollars had been generated. For the first time in years, they weren't struggling financially; they were thriving.

To Casey, it felt like relief. New money meant new projects, new committees, and fresh faces eager to take on governance responsibilities. He could play more golf, enjoy the expanding wine cellar, and reclaim Thursday Stag Days.

Once upon a time, Stag Day was legendary; cigars, strippers, and poker games with cash pots that rivaled car payments. The eighties softened that a bit after too many fights and a pickup truck slamming into a brick pillar at the front gate.

But one thing even the wives could never cut? The drinking. Bourbon, wine, beer, gin, and Stag Day flowed like a sacred river.

Casey intended to be first in line.

***

[FBI // ARKSTONE Field Deployment Note // 2025-04-15]

Subject: Garrot, Patrick (SA)

Cover Identity: Patrick "Pat" Garrot → Columbia View G&CC Food & Beverage Director

Justification: Role provides: Access to Board-level meetings (financial & vendor discussions). Authority over banquet/event cashflows (high money laundering risk). Daily proximity to membership cohort (including DTO-linked "new joiners"). Control of wine cellar & procurement channels (ideal surveillance choke point).

Status: Cover established—position accepted by unanimous Board vote.

***

The members believed the new Director was a lucky find: tall, square-jawed, polished without seeming pretentious, a former college golfer with a hospitality background, and skilled at working with people. A perfect fit.

What they didn't realize: Special Agent Patrick Garrot had been in the Bureau's hidden files since Medellín patterns started appearing on maps of the Pacific Northwest. ARKSTONE had pinpointed Columbia View as a crucial location months earlier.

As the Club's growth accelerated, Treasury's SAR logs lit up. Someone was using initiation fees as income and banquet spending as cover.

Garrot's new office sat between the kitchen and the boardroom, offering a perfect vantage point.

He had keys to the wine cellar, oversight of purchase orders, and a reason to review every invoice and every receipt that crossed the bar.

***

[NSA // COMINT // 2025-04-18 01:14:42Z]

Intercept: Encrypted WhatsApp → Medellín ISP

Text Extract (translated): "...the wine room is clean, the American signs the invoices. No eyes."

"...initiation fees launder faster than we thought.

Continue expansion. Correlation: Device ID matches Mariana González López, alias "Pearson."

***

From his first week, Garrot observed recurring patterns. New members in clean suits, handling illicit cash. Vendor invoices passing through shell distributors. A wine order that exceeds the needs of a 350-member Club threefold. The "culture" Casey Brookfield praised was exactly what ARKSTONE had predicted: DTO money shaping the Club's future, one Board vote at a time.

Brookfield, despite all his smiles, never asked the question that mattered. Who exactly were the new members, and why did they arrive all at once?

Pat Garrot didn't have to ask. His job was to listen, catalog, and wait.

At Cardiac Hill, Casey Brookfield was daydreaming about wine cellars and golf shots. Meanwhile, the man pouring that wine had already submitted his first coded report to Quantico.

***

[FBI // ARKSTONE Secure Cable // 2025-04-20]

Agent: SA   Garrot

Summary: Columbia View laundering operations confirmed. Front end: membership surge + initiation fees. Backend: banquet F&B spend, wine procurement   channel.

Recommendation: Maintain cover. Next step:

identify   Board   complicity   vs.   infiltration.

End Cable.

***

Hole #7 – "Gotcha Gulch" 339-yard Par 4

The boardroom clock ticked past 5:30. Casey Brookfield, still enjoying his shot on Cardiac Hill earlier, tapped his knuckles on the table and called the meeting to order. The goal was always to finish by 7:30. In reality, with this crowd, they were lucky to be done by 9:00.

Tonight's agenda was full: board rotations, officer elections, and committee reshuffles. Casey's term as president was nearing its end. He started with pleasantries, thanking outgoing members for their "service, your sentences, as it were." The room chuckled and applauded politely.

He began his introductions.

Larry Calhoun, tall and spindly, is more comfortable in a forest than in a crowd. The man played golf because he hated fishing. His doctoral advisor had pushed him into a "social sport." Larry found fairways tolerable; he still found people exhausting.

Next was Billy O'Connor, a man shaped like a keg and reeking of rancid fryer oil. Anyone with a functioning nose would quietly celebrate his departure.

Then Mr. Swan, once Dick, became "Richard," after buying a Porsche he couldn't drive. Swinger, creep, rumored pill-dropper. The staff whispered, and the members rolled their eyes. His term was ending, but his reputation wouldn't.

Carl Cliner was still in. Heavy drinker, great golfer, master electrician. Somehow kept his dignity even after ten Tito's and lemonades. His wife was beloved; Carl was tolerated with affection.

Amanda Clark hovered, eager yet unwelcome. A social climber, abrasive, self-proclaimed queen of the Women's Association. The staff had one word for her: "Karen."

Then Lisa Curtiss, glamorous and savvy, was the head of the House Committee. She managed Queen of Hearts, a Friday-night raffle whose pots sometimes topped $60,000. Her husband, Arnie, was a walking embarrassment, drunk and handsy, a liability the Club tolerated because Lisa was too valuable to offend.

Finally, Charlene Wright. A condescending, self-proclaimed expert on everything, with the body of a temptress and the face of a heavyweight fighter. Few wanted her in the room, and even fewer could tolerate her lectures.

The meeting would be another lengthy night of complaints, posturing, and polite applause.

But this time, one new face at the table wasn't just watching. He was recording.

***

[FBI // ARKSTONE Field Report // 2025-04-28]

Agent: SA Patrick Garrot (cover: Food & Beverage   Director)

Location: Columbia View G&CC Boardroom

Summary: Observed board composition + interpersonal dynamics. Outgoing members (Calhoun, O'Connor, Swan) reduce institutional memory. The incoming bloc appears overrepresented by "new money" members with unexplained   liquidity.

Flag: Potential DTO placement strategy—stacking governance via fast-tracked membership surge.

***

Garrot poured coffee as part of his cover. To the board, he was just the new Director: professional, attentive, able to discuss vintages and vendor contracts. But while he topped off mugs, he listened.

He recorded every financial phrase: wine cellar expansion, banquet revenue spike, committee fundraising. He observed who deferred to whom, who interrupted, and who exchanged glances across the table like coded signals.

Casey relied heavily on the membership surge's success: ninety new members, half a million in initiation fees. Everyone nodded, satisfied with the figures.

Garrot heard something else: velocity. No Club of this size, in a community as small as Columbia City, could triple its intake overnight. Not without help.

***

[Treasury Dept // FinCEN SAR EXTRACT // 2025-04-23]

Bank: Columbia River Community Bank Flagged Transfers: $2.5M aggregate, routed via shell LLCs (Montana, Nevada). Owners masked by BVI trusts. Destination:

Columbia View G&CC operating accounts.

Note: Unusual concentration in initiation fees.

Source liquidity is inconsistent with regional income brackets.

***

Amanda Clark couldn't help herself. She interrupted the discussion with comments about bylaws and Robert's Rules. Richard Swan smirked, whispered to Carl, and made everyone laugh. Casey held back a sigh.

Through it all, Garrot kept his cover intact, smiling, pouring, and taking mental notes. He noted Lisa Curtiss. Queen of Hearts wasn't just gambling; it was a cash magnet. A pot of $60,000 could be skimmed, padded, or "won" by someone the cartel already owned.

And he noted Amanda's ambition. The most dangerous infiltrators weren't always the most competent. Sometimes, DTOs used loud figures to draw attention, while others operated in the shadows.

***

[NSA // COMINT INTERCEPT // 2025-04-22   02:17Z]

Source: WhatsApp node, Medellín → Columbia City (device alias "Mariposa")

Extract:

"...tonight they move to vote. If our people control committees are in place, the F&B channel is clean. The American is blind."

Assessment: "American" likely refers to

Garrot cover. Confidence: MEDIUM. Dissemination to FBI ARKSTONE.

***

The meeting stretched into its second hour. Tempers flared slightly over the costs of expanding the wine cellar. Richard Swan insisted on "only premium imports." Larry Calhoun argued for local vendors. Amanda tried to insert herself into the procurement committee.

Garrot's cover role gave him final say on invoices. To the room, he was just a staffer. In truth, he now controlled the most sensitive laundering pipeline in the Club.

He looked around the table and realized that some of these people were just self-absorbed, petty, or drunk. But at least three, maybe four, were something different.

Not just members. Not just golfers. Assets.

***

[FBI // ARKSTONE Secure Cable // 2025-04-29]

Agent: SA   Garrot

Summary: Board composition compromised.

"New member" influx tied to DTO finance. F&B revenue channel confirmed as a vector for laundering. Gambling pot (Queen of Hearts) secondary   vector.

Recommendation: Authorize   HUMINT expansion. Suggest infiltration of the House Committee & audit of raffle proceeds. End Cable.

***

On Gotcha Gulch, a golfer aimed for a narrow fairway guarded by trees on both sides. One mis-hit, and you ended up in the ravine.

In the boardroom above that same gulch, Special Agent Patrick Garrot saw the line he had to play, one chance to make the shot. No mulligans.

Hole #8 – "Hungry Hollow" 371-yard Par 4

By the time Casey Brookfield transitioned from the old guard to the new, the boardroom had settled into a rhythm. Members half-listened, half-sipped, waiting for the break to arrive. But Special Agent Patrick Garrot, in his Food & Beverage Director cover, was wide awake.

The "new blood" had surged in since February, with ninety new members joining in less than six months. Tonight, the most prominent sat shoulder to shoulder, being introduced one after another.

Cal Worthington came first. A boutique investment firm owner, with a South American wife, possibly from Argentina, Chile, or Colombia, Casey hadn't been told.

The man's face had bronze undertones, his jaw was sharp, and his origin was unclear. His name was Anglo, but his story was less so.

Then David Hunt, with a lifeguard's appearance, swimmer's build, and deep green eyes that never quite met yours. A "technology consultant," working for "diverse international clients." Always remote, always vague. He disarmed skeptics with hand-drawn caricatures of staff and members, sketches that made people laugh while concealing the fact that he rarely spoke of himself.

Seated beside him was June Diago-Bransen, with her cherry-red hair, forty-seven but looking thirty-five.

She was the widow of a husband who had died "tragically" in South America while they were on vacation a few years earlier. Now, she's the president of the local community college. A power broker in academia, but to Garrot's eyes, just as helpful as any logistics manager.

Harry Phillips followed. Retired ship's captain with decades of experience handling Pacific ports, inbound machine parts, and outbound grain and lumber. A man who knew the rhythms of the river trade and every dock foreman by name. Reputation: hard worker, hard drinker, harder temper. His membership began in February, just as the laundering vector began to spike.

Doug Lynch was next. Painter. Galleries sold his landscapes across North and South America, and he spent years selling his work in Venezuela, Ecuador, and Colombia. Alex's wife had forced him to settle down, but his travel record looked like a map of a DTO courier. His gallery sales in Latin America alone justified a second look.

John Nash, in his mid-forties, is a storage-unit developer. An average man with average looks, but opportunistic. He built his fortune by buying cheap rural land along the I-5 corridor and flipping it for a profit. It's steady enough. However, his nomination for vice president later that evening showed he wasn't just average in ambition.

Finally, Barry Calderon. Cuban-born, Miami-raised, family escaped Castro in a fishing boat. Built a Caribbean-centered asset management firm into a 400-person powerhouse. Retired with wealth, connections, and a taste for yachts. His dartboard had landed him in Columbia City. A man who'd built careers moving money for displaced Cubans could move other money just as easily.

Casey called for a break. Members dispersed to bathrooms, the bar, or outside to smoke. Garrot lingered with a carafe of coffee, pretending to shuffle invoices. He didn't miss it: all of the new introductions huddled together in the corner, whispering, distinct from the rest of the room.

Odd, Casey thought. Obvious, Garrot knew.

***

[FBI // ARKSTONE Field Cable // 2025-05-01]

Agent: SA   Garrot

Location: Columbia View G&CC Boardroom

Observation: A new-member bloc (Worthington, Hunt, Diago-Bransen, Phillips, Lynch, Nash, Calderon) gathered apart from the other members during recess. Hushed conversation. Dispersed upon notice.

Assessment: DTO infiltration cell likely using "new member surge" as structured placement.

***

The elections made it official.

David Hunt was elected President, nominated by June Diago-Bransen and seconded by John Nash. Cal Worthington assumed the role of Vice President. Harry Phillips accepted the position of Secretary-Treasurer.

The remaining members were elected to the general board. A unified group now controlled Columbia View Golf & Country Club's boardroom. In less than six months, DTO-aligned assets had gained control of the key positions.

***

[CIA // SOUTHCOM Division // FLASH CABLE]

Target: "New Member Bloc – Columbia View G&CC"

Cross-Referencing: Hunt → multiple shell IT consultancies flagged by OFAC (Panama, Uruguay). Worthington → BVI-linked investment entity w/ cash surges post-Medellín seizures. Phillips → Maritime logs confirm frequent dock calls that overlap DTO shipments (1992–2018). Lynch → gallery sales in

Venezuela/Ecuador coincide with cash movement flagged by DEA Bogotá. Calderon → historical "clean" Cuban exile networks overlap with known DTO laundromats,   Miami   1990s.

Conclusion: Coordinated infiltration, not coincidence.

***

Amanda Clark chattered, Richard Swan leered, Lisa Curtiss eyed the raffle money. None of it mattered. The room had tilted.

To Casey Brookfield, it seemed like growth. To Patrick Garrot, it seemed as if the board had just been taken over.

The trap in Hungry Hollow was straightforward: you believed the fairway was wide until your drive ended up in a gulch you hadn't noticed from the tee.

Tonight, the Club got right into one.

***

[FBI // ARKSTONE Secure Cable // 2025-05-02]

Summary: Infiltration confirmed. Board majority controlled by DTO-aligned members.

Next Step: Monitor financial resolutions. Anticipate vector expansion for laundering through F&B, gambling, and port-linked contracts.

Directive: Maintain cover. Escalate HUMINT

penetration of the President (Hunt) + VP (Worthington).

Hole #9 – "Halfway Home" 303-yard Par 4

The applause echoed through the boardroom as David Hunt, now officially President, rose to thank Casey for his service. The cheers were heartfelt, and the bourbon was even warmer. Carl Cliner loudly muttered a "Thank God," prompting laughter, and just like that, leadership changed hands.

Casey remained behind the desk, volunteering to take the minutes. Hunt flipped through the agenda, eyes scanning the page. "Next: financials," he said.

Tom Douglas, the General Manager, stepped up to speak. He was polished, bronzed, charming, and looked like he could sell tequila in Cabo as easily as he managed a country club in SW Washington.

Seven years ago, he had 'inherited' the Club as a financial disaster: delinquent members, overdue loans, and COD deliveries. He'd cleaned house and stabilized the place. Now, with the membership surge, he was boasting.

"Eighty-one new members in ninety days," Tom said, tapping the printed P&L. "That's thirty-five percent growth. $120,000 in monthly revenue. More than $400,000 in initiation fees."

The cheer was deafening. Board members patted each other on the backs, glasses lifted high. For the first time in ten years, Columbia View appeared solvent.

Pat Garrot, in his role as Food & Beverage Director, smiled along with the others. Inside, he made a mental note. Money flowing in at this velocity was less of a miracle and more of an anomaly.

***

[FBI // ARKSTONE Analyst Note // 2025-05-08]

Subject: Columbia View G&CC Financials. Initiation revenue spike: $400k in <90 days. Pattern matches DTO wash-through vectors (high initiation, low churn). Probability laundering: 0.81 (HIGH). Directive: SA Garrot to initiate vendor-audit observation. Priority: incoming shipments (wine/spirits).

***

The general meeting adjourned at nine. Members dispersed, leaving only the new Board for the executive session. They stayed past midnight, voices muffled through the wood-paneled door. Capital projects included a $10 million rebuild. A missed vote eight years ago had cost them seven million in inflation. Hunt wanted to revive the project, expand the south property, and buy out houses on Holly Drive.

On paper, it seemed ambitious. To Garrot, it looked like a laundering scale.

***

[NSA // COMINT // 2025-05-09 04:11Z]

Intercept: WhatsApp → Medellín node

Text (translated): "...the Americans talk of a new pool, new courts. Good. They need big numbers. Move the next shipment as wine, cases of reserve. He signs   the   invoices."

Assessment: Reference = SA Garrot cover.

***

Two mornings later, the shipment arrived. A white panel truck, unmarked except for a magnetic decal: Willamette Select Distributors. The paperwork listed 12 cases of Chilean Malbec as a special order for the wine cellar expansion.

Garrot was in the loading bay with a clipboard. To anyone watching, he was doing his job: verifying invoices and initialing line items.

He lifted a case. Too heavy. A twelve-bottle crate of Malbec should weigh about forty-five pounds. This one was closer to seventy. He made a mental note, smiled at the driver, and signed the delivery sheet.

Later, alone in the cellar, he pried back a corner of cardboard. Inside, bottles—corked, labeled, and legitimate. He weighed one in his hand, nearly two pounds heavier than it should be. Two pounds of $100 bills would be about $90,000. Twelve bottles are worth over a million dollars. Twelve cases, that was real money.

He scraped the foil neck capsule with his fingernail. Beneath the shrinkwrap, the glass was thicker than usual—double-walled. He tapped the bottle gently against a shelf, quiet and dense. Then he turned it over and held it to the cellar's light. Liquid sloshed inside, but not all of it was wine.

***

[FBI // ARKSTONE Field Report // 2025-05-11]

Agent: SA   Garrot

Location: Columbia View G&CC – Wine Cellar

Observation: Chilean Malbec bottles are double-walled. Approx. 2lb excess weight/bottle. Visual confirmation of secondary chamber (non-wine).

Assessment: DTO concealment method for currency or narcotics micro-shipment.

Action: Maintained cover. Logged shipment in inventory as received. Requesting technical support for a non-intrusive bottle scan.

***

Above him, in the Boardroom, members debated adding tennis and pickleball courts. To them, Alder Creek was just another hole on the course, another par four where drives disappeared into the alder stands.

To Garrot, it was the first confirmed shipment, proof that the DTO had roots in the Club's cellar.

And in the quiet of the wine racks, he whispered the truth to himself:

Gotcha.

Hole #10 – "Alder Creek" 394-yard Par 4

Four weeks later, a Friday night delivered the kind of spectacle Columbia View hadn't seen in years. A high-profile fundraiser with wine, music, and money. The dining hall shone with rented chandeliers. The parking lot overflowed with luxury SUVs and German sedans from as far away as

Portland. Board members preened like peacocks, basking in the glow of their newfound relevance.

Upstairs, guests sipped Malbec and Sauvignon Blanc. Downstairs, in the wine cellar, the Bureau was working.

Special Agent Patrick Garrot played his role perfectly.

To the members, he was the new F&B Director, personally managing the evening. Polished, attentive, a man who understood alcohol and caterers. He smiled, poured drinks, and charmed donors. He also wore a Bluetooth earpiece tuned to a frequency no one else in the building could hear.

***

[FBI // QRT INSERTION LOG // 2025-05-18 20:42Z]

Operation   Codename: *Cellar   Sweep*

Team: 3x QRT (Quick Reaction Tech) specialists,   1x   ASAC   observer

Entry: Service tunnel, east side maintenance access

Tasking: Non-intrusive scan of 14 Malbec cases (suspected DTO concealment bottles). Deploy miniaturized   TeraHertz   imager   +   acoustic tomography   wand.

ROE: No bottle breach. Covertness absolute. Abort if member/board access is <15m away.

***

The Board's leadership moved around like conquering generals. David Hunt, the new President, shook hands at every table, smiling proudly. Cal Worthington, Vice President, mingled with the investment crowd. Harry Phillips, Secretary-Treasurer, shared shipping stories with anyone holding a glass.

Together, they moved through the fundraiser like a formation. To Garrot, it was confirmation. The bloc wasn't improvising anymore; they were commanding.

"Pat," Lisa Curtiss called, beckoning him toward the raffle table. "Queen of Hearts pulls at ten. You'll want to see this."

"Of course," Garrot smiled, excusing himself from a group of donors. He walked calmly, but his pulse raced faster inside his chest. He knew what else was happening, directly beneath his feet.

***

[QRT TECH FEED // LIVE // 20:57Z]

Scan   Result   Case   #4:

Bottle density anomaly → secondary chamber detected.   Fill   ~82%   solid   particulate.

Chemical Sniff: THz resonance matches the ink trace   markers   on   U.S.   currency.

Prelim Estimate: $1.2M USD in concealed notes.

Case Status: Flagged.

***

Garrot refilled glasses, nodded at jokes, and received praise for the Chilean selections. His eyes remained calm, hiding what he knew: the wine in circulation tonight was cover, but the real vintage was cash. Millions, concealed in bottles, stacked neatly in the racks below.

Amanda Clark cornered him mid-service, voice shrill with self-importance. "Patrick, I don't think the dessert wines are balanced properly with the soufflé course. I've studied this, you know..."

Garrot smiled professionally. "Thank you, Amanda. I'll make a note."

His earpiece buzzed.

Scan complete. Fourteen cases are positive. Currency concealed. Extraction impossible tonight. Any advice?

He walked toward the kitchen, cover intact, whispering just above a hum of clattering pans. "Maintain. Inventory logged. Next pickup window?"

"Driver ETA: Wednesday. Same vendor. Same channel."

***

[FBI // ARKSTONE OPS ROOM – PORTLAND]

Live feed glowed on monitors. Analysts cross-matched the distributor decal, *Willamette Select Distributors*, to a shell entity linked to Panama filings.

Treasury's SAR flagged $2.1M in outbound wire transfers the same week.

"They're staging the wash," one analyst muttered. "Wine in, cash out. Club's the rinse cycle."

The ASAC leaned over. "Garrot holds the position until Wednesday. We want the driver. The crate's worthless without the courier."

***

Back in the hall, raffle tickets were being drawn. Applause erupted as the Queen of Hearts pot carried over, still without a winner. The crowd laughed, clapped, and ordered more drinks. Upstairs, it was just another good night at a private Club.

Downstairs, Garrot knew the DTO had already made it halfway home. And unless he played his line perfectly, so had he.

***

[FBI // ARKSTONE SECURE CABLE // 2025-05-19]

Summary: 14 cases scanned. Currency confirmed. Est. $1.2M. Distribution channel confirmed DTO-linked.

Next Step: Controlled intercept of vendor pickup. Status: Cover maintained.

Hole #11 – "Columbia View" 289-yard Par 4

Four weeks earlier, Pat Garrot left his coded voicemail for "Mom and Dad." The Bureau had long since set up the line as a dead drop, but the message tone remained domestic, banal. It was intended to be that way.

Hey, Mom, and hi Dad... I took the F&B Manager position at the country club in Columbia City. I started a few weeks ago... love you both.

The moment he hung up, ARKSTONE servers in Quantico logged the time, encrypted the file, and flagged it for review.

In an hour, his handler would call his secondary phone, the one sealed in a fireproof safe beneath his floorboards. That phone never rang for social reasons.

By the time Hazel Mae was tugging him around Crescent Lake, the call came through. The Bureau's voice was crisp, warm, and authoritative.

"Pat, good to hear from you," Henry Osborne said. "Sounds like we're moving quickly toward phase two."

"Yes indeed," Garrot said, smiling as if the words were casual, though his pulse betrayed him.

Phase two was the intercept.

***

[FBI // ARKSTONE OPS ORDER // 2025-05-22]

Codename: *Columbia View / Halfway House*

Objective: Controlled intercept of DTO cash courier.

Target: "Willamette Select Distributors" panel truck, scheduled pickup 05/24 10:00. Load: 14 cases Malbec (double-walled currency concealment). Deployment: FBI Portland Field + DEA Tactical (undercover freight inspectors). Cover: SA Garrot to facilitate routine cellar release. Maintain plausible deniability.

***

For two years, Garrot meticulously built his cover. He crafted restaurant résumés, appeared at trade shows, secured MAST and food handler permits, and even did grunt work at a riverfront bar where the owners cared more about table turnover than quality. All to convincingly pose as a food-and-beverage professional tired of Seattle, seeking pace and purpose.

Now, the role gave him precisely what the Bureau needed: unrestricted access to the wine cellar and food stores, as well as the authority to accept and sign for shipments. The Board believed they had hired a professional. In reality, they had let an FBI strike team into the building through the kitchen door.

***

Friday morning began with coastal fog rolling up the Columbia River. By nine-thirty, Garrot was in the cellar, clipboard in hand, logging bottles by lot number. Upstairs, members laughed over breakfast mimosas.

At 9:58, a white panel truck eased into the loading bay, with the same decal as before: *Willamette Select Distributors.* The driver stepped out in jeans and a flannel shirt, holding a clipboard. He looked like a man delivering produce to a school cafeteria.

Garrot shook his hand, casual, smiling. "Morning. Running on time today."

The man grinned. "Better than traffic."

To any camera, to any passerby, it was business as usual. To Garrot, the coded phrase meant *the load is hot.*

He signed the manifest, marking the cases for return. Behind him, his Bluetooth earpiece whispered alive.

"Target confirmed. All units in play."

***

[DEA Tactical Log // 2025-05-24 10:04Z]

Action: Panel truck intercepted 2.4 miles from Columbia   View   on   River   Road.

Tactic: Oregon State Police cover stop (broken taillight pretext).

Result: Driver detained. Vehicle searched under warrant. 14 Malbec cases recovered.

Contents: Approx. $1.2M USD concealed currency. Packaging matched the Medellín DTO method.

Status: Driver in federal custody, vehicle impounded.

***

In the cellar, Garrot closed his clipboard after the driver drove off. Upstairs, Lisa Curtiss was arranging raffle tickets for Queen of Hearts.

By ten-fifteen, the Bureau had the truck. By ten-thirty, the DTO's courier was on his way to a secure facility.

By eleven, the wine cellar at Columbia View looked exactly as it had before, with empty racks waiting for bottles that would never arrive.

Garrot went upstairs into the noise of brunch chatter, smiling politely as Amanda Clark cornered him about the "future of dessert wines." He listened, nodded, and let her talk.

Beneath his calm exterior, the situation had changed. Columbia View was no longer just a golf course; it had become a battlefield.

And the first shot had just been fired.

***

[FBI // ARKSTONE SECURE CABLE // 2025-05-24]

Summary: Intercept successful. $1.2M seized. Courier   detained.

Next Step: DTO will note missing funds within 48 hours.

Expect an internal probe and replacement courier. Cover at Columbia View remains uncompromised.

Directive: SA Garrot maintain role. Monitor Board reaction. Prepare Phase Three escalation.

***

On the course, Hole #11 was short, just 289 yards. Tempting to try and drive the green, easy to overplay, and end up in trouble.

The Bureau had made its shot. Clean contact. Now it was rolling toward the pin.

Hole #12 – "Hookers Hollow" 346-yard Par 4

Pat Garrot slipped a crow's feather into the spine of his book, Advanced Chemistry for Bakers. He grinned, technical science written like a novel, a mix of *The Martian* and *Caffeine*.

His cup was empty. He stood to refill it. One more cup of fuel before the shower, before the day begins, and before stepping back into the role of the Club's Food & Beverage Director. The man with the keys to the cellar.

But beneath the simple ritual, his mind was elsewhere. Placement. Layering. Integration. The Bureau's white-collar playbook was ingrained in him.

Laundering wasn't just dirty money slipping into tills; it was empire-building through subtraction and disguise.

And somewhere above him, the empire was starting to realize that one of its shipments had gone missing.

***

At First National, teller Sarah Gunderson flipped a deposit slip. "Country Club's on a roll," she said to Michelle. "Bigger every week. Cash, too."

Michelle nodded, recalling the loan committee's notes. "Paid off their operating loan. Seventeen months early."

They smiled, small-town proud. But the note reached the Bureau's Portland fusion center within 24 hours: paid-off debt, cash-heavy deposits. The integration phase was underway.

***

[FBI // ARKSTONE FIELD CABLE // 2025-05-29]

Subject: Columbia   View   G&CC

Observation: Operating loan retired early (17mo). Cash deposits are increasing in frequency/volume.

Assessment: Integration phase advancing. Probability of DTO suspicion over missing courier funds   =   HIGH.

Directive: SA Garrot maintain close-in HUMINT. Monitor Board-level discussions for signs of internal probe.

***

Vendors also noticed. Bill O'Shea, with twenty years of experience selling paper products, grinned like a lottery winner after Columbia View placed its third order in a single quarter, the largest yet. His boss congratulated him; the sales floor cheered loudly. No one asked why a Club of 350 members was suddenly using supplies as if it were a resort twice its size.

At McNary Golf Club, Head Pro Perry Phillips fumed as Columbia View poached two assistants: they received moving stipends, rent-subsidized apartments, and 20% pay raises. "Happy horseshit," he spat.

His GM agreed. They couldn't compete, and they couldn't explain how a once-struggling club suddenly had cash for signing bonuses.

***

Upstairs, DTO leadership was restless.

President David Hunt called a private meeting. Vice President Cal Worthington leaned forward, voice low but firm. "One of our couriers went missing. Shipment never cleared."

Harry Phillips, Secretary-Treasurer, scowled. "A million two doesn't just vanish. Either Customs got lucky, or someone on this side of the river is playing both ends."

"Could be sloppy paperwork," Hunt said, but his tone lacked conviction.

Worthington's gaze shifted. "Then we test our people. Accounts, managers... even new hires. Anyone with access to inventory."

No one mentioned Garrot's name. Not yet. But he felt the pressure building like steam rising through the floorboards.

***

[DEA // SOUTHCOM COMINT EXCERPT // 2025-05-28   03:14Z]

Intercept: Medellín node → Oregon

"...the wine was signed, but the money is gone. If the Americans touched it, we have a traitor inside. Test them. Watch the new man."

Assessment: "New man" likely refers to SA Garrot cover. Confidence: HIGH.

***

For Jhon Jairo Gonzalez, this was no accident. His empire had been built on patience and precision:

scholarships fueling talent pipelines into Fortune 500 companies, integration strategies disguised as philanthropy.

But Mariana's plan, membership-owned clubs, was the shortcut he had dreamed of. Six months in, and millions were already flowing through Columbia View.

Now, the shortcut revealed its first sign of weakness.

***

In laundering, placement was straightforward: cash to the till, invoices to the ledger. Layering was an art, weaving transactions through vendors, payroll, and suppliers. But integration was essential for survival. It was how the money was returned, clean and untouchable.

And when integration faltered, suspicion became oxygen. It burned through trust, through cover, through men like Garrot.

***

In Hookers Hollow, golfers were tempted to drive the green because of its short distance. Most ended up slicing into the trees, caught in the dogleg's deception.

At Columbia View, the DTO made its own hook shot. And the man holding the club, Special Agent Pat Garrot, knew they were beginning to search for him.

Hole #13 – "Big Bend" 504-yard par 5

Pat sat at his home desk, facing the wide picture window to the west, a dog-eared paperback in his hands. The book had traveled with him through three moves, two assignments, and countless nights of studying. The edges were frayed, the spine cracked like an old river rock.

It was late, nearly 10 PM, and he had been home just over an hour after a twelve-hour day at the Club. Outside the glass, mainly was blackness: no moon, no stars, only the distant headlights of cars and trucks speeding along the freeway. But Pat's mind was alert, bright, and sharp. A plan was beginning to take shape.

The title across the faded cover read _Games and Decisions_, published in 1957 by R. Duncan Luce and Howard Raiffa. Game theory in its modern form had existed for more than fifty years before this book, but this was where it had been distilled, formalized, and expanded. Pat had read it cover to cover at least six times, enough that his first copy had disintegrated into loose pages.

This second copy had already started down the same path.

Henry Wellborne, his boss, shared his obsession. Over the years, they had spent countless hours analyzing strategies, modeling outcomes, and drawing chalkboard diagrams of opponents as if they were chess pieces.

The Bureau had learned to apply game theory in its investigations, and Pat and Henry had been early advocates. It wasn't a tool to display. It was a discipline, a way of understanding how players move when the rules are unseen.

Game theory is fundamentally simple: it studies decision-making where outcomes depend on your choices and others'. Players, each with their own goals, consider strategies, anticipate moves, and calculate payoffs. Whether they realize it or not, they are engaged in playing.

The truth is, everyone starts learning the basics as a child. Tag. Hopscotch. Tic-tac-toe. Chutes and Ladders. Even "Go Fish."

A thousand games from many cultures, each teaching a lesson in interaction. The first experience of offense and defense. That's when the framework begins to take shape: if I do this, they'll do that. If I wait, maybe I win. The rules may be simple, but the patterns are universal.

The first pillars are Players and Strategies. Players are the decision-makers; strategies are the actions they can take. Next come Payoffs and Utilities: the rewards, satisfactions, and consequences of each move. In economics, that means money. In politics, power. In crime, survival.

Then there's the equilibrium, the point at which no player has any incentive to change their strategy, because doing so wouldn't improve the outcome. It's stability in chaos. Nash called it equilibrium, but in reality, it was like a psychological trench line... move at your own risk.

Once, these ideas were limited to board games and military drills. Today, the internet reaches everywhere. Fields such as economics, business, politics, biology, and law all use it. Auction houses rely on it to estimate bids. Political campaigns analyze it to find voting blocs. Biologists use it to simulate predator-prey interactions. Even evolution itself can be seen as a game in which successful strategies are copied, and failures fade away.

Pat thumbed through the pages and stopped at the Prisoner's Dilemma. Two suspects, two cells, no communication. They can cooperate and stay silent or betray each other for personal gain. The paradox: cooperation leads to the best group outcome, but betrayal offers a higher personal payoff. Rationality conflicts with self-interest. That tension between the individual and the collective was the heartbeat of human conflict.

Evolutionary games followed, with strategies shifting over time like sandbars in a river. Auction theory, in turn, suggests that markets and bidders maneuver like hawks circling over prey. The applications were endless.

And now, here he was, an undercover operative deep inside a labyrinthine organization, surrounded by law enforcement partners, all of them players in overlapping games—some allies, some predators, some wearing masks thicker than his own. Game theory wasn't a curiosity for Pat; it was survival.

***

The Board of Directors wasted no time. With the ink barely dry on their appointments, they turned the Club's growing revenues into tools for expansion. Their first action: pass an amendment to the bylaws.

No longer would million-dollar decisions need full membership approval.

Now the Board could sign contracts, spend up to two million dollars, and commit the Club to obligations with just a few signatures.

The vote to approve it was perfunctory, conducted by mail and email. The outcome was never in doubt. The process had been rigged well before the ballots were sent.

Their first project was cosmetic but costly: new cart paths. Nearly $1.5 million worth. A four-month timeline, though everyone in the room knew construction projects often face delays; permits, demolitions, sourcing materials, and the never-ending search for contractors who are both skilled and available. October at the earliest, maybe November. By then, the playing season would be over.

But the paths were only the initial step. The Board's focus was on bigger projects. Architects and engineers were already sketching plans for a redesigned clubhouse. Locker rooms were gutted and rebuilt. A new Pro Shop, pool, and storage facilities were also planned. Early estimates ranged from $7 million to $10 million. And Pat knew from long Bureau experience: every project ran over budget, every schedule slipped, and every promise of "on time and under cost" ended in laughter.

Pat leaned back from the book, his mind racing on two levels. On the surface, a golf club is changing its look; beneath the surface, a series of moves and counter-moves, investments and contracts, each step another stone in the road.

The Board wasn't just beautifying the Club; they were consolidating control, centralizing authority, and most importantly, creating channels for money to flow, shift, and vanish into concrete, asphalt, and architectural renderings.

It was, in game theory terms, a multi-level contest. The visible game was construction, while the invisible one controlled the resources. In both cases, the equilibrium point had not yet been reached.

Pat gently closed the book, the feathered edges whispering against each other. Outside, the night stayed black, and the window reflected only his own face. The plan forming in his mind wasn't complete, but he had the pieces. Players. Strategies. Payoffs.

The Board thought they were just playing a simple upgrade game. But they hadn't yet realized who else was at the table.

Hole #14 – "The Deceiver" 122-yard par 3

Jeffery Phillips gently eased his Toyota Land Cruiser into a spot at the very southern end of the clubhouse parking lot. He could have parked closer, but the extra distance offered a buffer and some anonymity. From this vantage point, he could observe the comings and goings without drawing attention to himself.

He killed the engine, leaned down, and lifted his pant leg. The small Kimber K6s revolver slid into its holster above his ankle with the ease of habit. A tool, nothing more. He grabbed a manila folder from the passenger seat, the thin, fabricated history that would pass for his résumé. His cover story, condensed into two pages.

Jeff stepped out, locked the vehicle with a quiet chirp, and checked his reflection in the mirror: white teeth, dark hair, youthful face. At twenty-seven, he still looked like he might be carded at a bar, which made him perfect for roles that required him to blend in with younger staff. Satisfied, he smiled at himself, a practiced but genuine gesture, and began the two-hundred-yard walk to the front entrance.

As he walked, his mind replayed the résumé. A boy from Walla Walla, Washington. Years in hospitality. Line cook at fourteen. Country club snack shack by seventeen. Serving members at the pool and courts. Just enough truth woven into the fiction to pass any casual check. His hospitality background added credibility, the kind that gave weight to a handshake and eye contact across an interview table.

Jeff wasn't nervous. He didn't need to be. The interview was with Pat Garrot, who already knew exactly who he was.

***

Pat unlocked the outer office door with practiced ease. He enjoyed being first. The calm of the clubhouse before the rush of members and staff brought a sense of clarity. By 8:30, he was at his desk, the only light on in the administrative suite.

The lock on his office door yielded to another key, one of only two that opened it. He and Tom Douglas, the general manager, carried master keys; no one else did. Pat stepped inside, turned on the overhead light, and headed straight to the closet.

The Glock 21 went into the biometric safe, the steel door sealing with a muted click. In Southwest Washington, firearms were common enough, but Club policy prohibited alcohol and handguns on the same dance floor. There is no need to test that particular rule.

At his desk, Pat powered up the computer and opened his calendar. Six interviews were scheduled in half-hour blocks. Three real applications, three Bureau plants. "Team Garrot," he thought, a private grin at the name. Soon, he'd have intelligence coverage integrated into every shift of the Club's operations.

No single person could stay on site for twelve to fourteen hours without raising suspicion.

However, three agents, rotated cleverly, could offer almost continuous observation.

With this coverage, opportunities arose to place microphones, cameras, and collection points. Each device was like a stone on the Go board, positioned not for immediate victory but for long-term strategic advantage.

His first interview, Jeff Phillips, was scheduled for 9:30. Plenty of time to make coffee. Managers arriving would expect it. Service-disguised surveillance; that was the lesson.

As the pot hissed and gurgled behind the bar, Pat considered angles; cameras required both concealment and sight lines. Microphones demanded proximity without visibility.

The lounge, the restaurant, the hallways. They were nodes in a network waiting to be mapped. He poured his coffee, added cream, and carried it into the dining area.

Sliding into a corner six-top, he faced the room as though he were a member evaluating the ambiance. He scanned walls, soffits, and artwork.

Where would a lens vanish without a shadow? Where could a microphone be tucked beneath molding or under a table lip? If interrupted, he had his ready alibi: every good manager inspects from the guest's perspective. Cleanliness. Lines of sight. Atmosphere. No one would question it.

Pat glanced at his watch. Almost time. He'd need a golf cart to take the candidate on a "course tour," privacy wrapped in professionalism. He stood up and headed to the Pro Shop.

***

Jeff approached the clubhouse doors with his file in hand, posture relaxed, expression open. But beneath the practiced youthful demeanor, his mind was strategizing. Players and tactics. Every step in this process was a calculated move. He was about to sit across from Pat, his handler, but in the eyes of the rest of the Club, he'd seem like a stranger applying for a job. He would need to play that role perfectly.

Game theory illustrated the situation clearly: in any information contest, deception was a key tactic. A cover résumé was not just a piece of paper; it was a carefully constructed payoff matrix. Every fact, whether included or omitted, shifted the opponent's calculations. Members, staff, and even management all played against him, though they didn't realize it. Some might test him with small questions, while others might probe more deeply. As long as his answers matched the fiction, the equilibrium would hold.

The "Deceiver" was more than just a hole on the golf course. It represented Jeff himself, embodying the paradox of truth hidden behind lies, a twenty-seven-year-old FBI agent disguised as a kid looking for a job.

***

In the kitchen of a modest house not far from the Club, John Nash, the namesake of equilibrium itself, was dicing onions and peppers. He slid them into hot oil, lowered the flame, and set the tomatoes to blanch. He wasn't the mathematician who had formalized balance in games of strategy, but his daily cooking reflected the same discipline: ingredients as players, flavors as payoffs, timing as equilibrium. Too much heat, and the game tilted toward bitterness. Too little, and it collapsed into blandness.

Nash's quiet domestic routine highlighted the reality that Pat and Jeff were experiencing. Every interaction, every plan, and every deception formed a pattern, with balance as the ultimate aim.

Back at the Club, as Jeff walked through the entrance and Pat headed toward the Pro Shop, two players moved to their next plays. The board was set. The game was underway.

Hole #15 – "Hidden Green" 412-yard par 4

The soldiers arrived quietly, not in convoys or making any noise that would draw attention, but alone, in different cars, at various hours, seamlessly blending into the city's rhythm. The Bureau didn't move in formation unless necessary. Here, subtlety was their main advantage.

Pat had taken over a small room downstairs beneath the Club's administrative wing. No windows, no blinds to close. The room smelled faintly of dust and whiteboard cleaner, with the air conditioning turning on in uneven bursts.

Against one wall was what looked like a relic from another time: a sheet of heavy cardboard propped on a stand, covered in photographs, photocopies, receipts, and handwritten notes.

Cliché or not, he had threaded pushpins and string across it all; red, blue, and green, linking faces to names, invoices to projects, timelines to outcomes. It wasn't just showmanship. The visual web clarified patterns in a way digital spreadsheets could not.

The agents he had started to gather, his "soldiers," sat around the table. Jeff Phillips was present, still in the crisp uniform shirt the Club had issued him just days earlier.

Two others, Maria Torres and Kevin Dunn, new hires in the lounge and kitchen, leaned forward, eyes sharp. They were young, driven, and aware of the stakes.

Pat stood at the board holding a black marker. He gently tapped the marker against his palm, like a metronome for the briefing.

"This is not a game of speed," he said, his voice steady. "It's a game of position. You don't win a par four by smashing the ball off the tee into the trees. You win it by placement. Shot one puts you in position. Shot two takes you to the green. The green is hidden right now. That's why we're here."

The metaphor lingered in the air, and he let it.

***

The photos showed members of the Board of Directors, their spouses, contractors, and bankers.

Pushpins connected the Board president, a man named Harold "Hal" Whitcomb, to a series of Delaware-registered shell companies. Another pin linked those companies to bids submitted for construction projects at the Club. Yet another pin directed to wire transfers that vanished into accounts with overseas routing numbers.

Kevin leaned in and asked, "So the cart path project… it isn't just about cart paths?"

Pat shook his head. "No. Cart paths are covered. They're the rough on the edge of the fairway.

The real play is in the contracts. Money flows in, gets laundered through inflated invoices, then disappears into shells. By the time anyone notices, it will be too late. And Whitcomb and his friends can smile and say delays, cost overruns, material shortages, just construction realities. Who's going to argue?"

Maria tapped one of the photos with her pen. "What about this guy, Feldman? The architect?"

Feldman's a player, but not one of the captains," Pat said. "He gets his cut, sure. But he's not steering the strategy. He's a pawn who thinks he's a bishop. Our job is to observe the real moves if we catch pawns, good. But the king and queen are what really matter."

When I was a young golfer, an old pro explained it to me this way," Pat continued. "Your average golfer will stand over his ball, looking at his approach shot and planning to hit the green. A low handicapper might picture hitting the same shot but aiming for a tree or bush in their line of sight. A professional, however, will see the same bush, and their target will be a specific leaf.

Jeff spoke up, his voice calm. "That means equilibrium hasn't been reached yet. They're still playing, but not aggressively... yet. That leaves openings."

Pat nodded. "Exactly. They think the green is invisible to us. But every hidden green has a line of sight if you know where to look."

***

The meeting ran into the afternoon, with agents rotating in and out to ensure no one was away from their posts for too long. Amid discussions about schedules and cover stories, Pat detailed the placement of surveillance equipment. Maria would oversee the women's locker room and poolside areas, Kevin was responsible for the kitchen and service hallways, and Jeff covered the lounges and bar.

Each was reminded that concealment involved not just physical things but also behavior. A wire under a table could be accidentally discovered. A camera above a door might be noticed. But the bigger risk was attracting suspicion themselves.

Members at the Club were predators hiding behind the guise of patrons; one slip could lead to scrutiny.

"Remember," Pat said, circling back to the board, "they don't know they're in a game. That's our advantage. If they don't realize they're playing, they won't change strategies. And that makes them predictable."

***

Later, when the meeting ended and the agents dispersed, Pat stayed behind. He looked at the web of lines on the board. From a distance, it resembled the tangled rough of a golf course map; fairways winding, bunkers marked, hazards outlined. But unlike a golf course, the hazards here were human.

He reached out and tugged on a single thread, the line connecting Whitcomb to a contractor named Samuels. The pin shifted slightly. That was the flaw in every web; pull one line, and the whole thing trembles. Somewhere in those connections lay the shot that would open the view to the hidden green.

Pat took a sip from his now-cold coffee and sat down heavily at the table.

He thought back to Luce and Raiffa, to Nash, and to all the nights he'd spent analyzing models of cooperation and betrayal. The Board was living through a version of the Prisoner's Dilemma every day. They could all cooperate, launder smoothly, stay silent, and profit.

But greed made betrayal tempting. Sooner or later, one of them would think the payoff was better by flipping. His job was to recognize when that moment came and to be ready with the microphone on.

***

That evening, as twilight dimmed the windows, Pat walked around the perimeter of the clubhouse. He paused at the tee box, gazing down the fairway. Hole #15, played longer than it appeared, had a narrow landing zone, a dogleg left, and a green tucked just out of sight. Many golfers made the mistake of swinging for distance and ended up in the trees. The smart ones laid up short, took the dogleg angle, and trusted their second shot.

Pat exhaled slowly. That was his strategy now: lay up, take position. The green might be hidden, but it was there, waiting.

He pictured the Board members as golfers on this hole. Some swung blindly, chasing distance and focusing only on the immediate reward. Others were cautious, trying to stay on the fairway but unaware of the trap near the green. None suspected that someone else was already planning their shots, mapping their choices, and predicting where the ball would land.

***

Back inside, he packed his bag and turned off the computer. The cardboard stayed propped in the corner, the threads crisscrossing like the lines of an unfinished course map.

The soldiers had arrived. The team was in position. The camouflage was hidden, yes. But not forever.

Pat turned off the lights, locked the door, and stepped into the dark hallway. Tomorrow, the game would go on. With each move, the way to the hidden green would become clearer.

Hole #16 – "Coffin Rock" 438-yard par 4

The clubhouse remodel was presented to the members as modernization: a fresh boost of prestige for a property already rich in status. The renderings displayed sleek locker rooms, expanded dining areas, and a new Pro Shop with oak counters and glass cases. Members smiled, signed checks, and trusted the Board.

But behind the drywall and polished tile, hidden spaces began to take shape. Construction crews, most of them unaware, built more than they realized. Underneath the stairs in the northwest wing, a walk-in humidor stretched wide enough to impress even the most demanding cigar aficionado.

Adjacent to it, a climate-controlled wine cellar offered racks for vintages few could pronounce. Both were real. Both would be toured and admired by members.

What no one but a select few understood was that each room contained secrets. Behind a panel in the humidor, a hidden cavity ran the length of the wall. It was large enough to hold duffels of cash, cases of negotiable bonds, or velvet pouches heavy with stones. In the wine cellar, one rack pivoted smoothly when pressure was applied to a specific bottle. Behind it, a steel door disguised as masonry opened into a secure chamber.

These weren't just luxuries; they were vaults. The cartel insisted on having them.

Jon José, one of the managing partners of the laundering operation, had a fondness for rubies and emeralds. Diamonds were too obvious and easily flagged at customs or pawn networks. Colored stones moved with less suspicion, their value often underestimated by outsiders. His collection, accumulated from shipments ferried through the

Club, had grown into something more like a private museum.

Deliveries came like clockwork. A black Escalade here, a contractor's truck there. A man unloading wine crates, another carrying golf bags; each hiding something in plain sight.

Drops were scheduled during lulls in member activity, early mornings or evenings when the dining room had cleared. Cartel members blended in as maintenance crews, couriers, or service staff.

The handoffs were precise. A cooler of fish for the kitchen might hold shrink-wrapped bricks of cash. A wine shipment could hide velvet bags. The goods would be logged, stored, and later moved into secret vaults until pickup time.

Pickups were equally clean. An agent pretending to be a deliveryman wheeled out a case, nodded at a Board member or trusted lieutenant, and left before anyone thought twice.

Additionally, for insurance reasons, security cameras covered every part of the Club: hallways, lounges, kitchens, and loading docks. What the membership didn't realize was that the system didn't just record the feeds; they were also mirrored and streamed quietly to cartel monitors in safe houses as far away as Colombia. Every move, every delivery, every handoff was watched.

The irony wasn't lost on Pat. The cartel's eyes now rivaled his own. His team had started placing their own listening devices and pinhole cameras, weaving intelligence into the same web the criminals believed they controlled. Two games layered over each other on the same board, with neither side fully aware of the other's pieces.

***

That afternoon, Pat walked along the service hallway that connected the main dining room to the loading dock. His pace was relaxed, coffee cup in hand, but his eyes observed every detail. He paused at a new camera mounted near the ceiling, its lens directed at the junction where the hallways met. It was small, black, and unmarked. Not a Club installation.

He tilted his head, thinking. Golfers who played Hole #16 knew the landing zone was tricky.

From the tee, the fairway looked wide, but a granite outcrop, Coffin Rock, sat right in the middle.

Shots aimed directly often ricocheted or were buried. Only by playing the angle and skirting wide could a golfer find safety.

The camera was Coffin Rock. Too obvious to ignore, but too risky to confront directly. To handle it properly, Pat would need to angle carefully.

He went back to his 'secret' office, closed the door, and updated his board. A new thread connected Whitcomb to José, then to construction invoices, and finally to the hidden rooms. Another string links to photographs from the cameras.

Jeff arrived in mid-afternoon, still wearing his busboy apron. He sat down in a chair across from Pat and lowered his voice.

"I've got confirmation from the lounge. Two guys, not staff, doing a delivery last night. Kitchen door. They rolled in a case of cabernet. The sommelier swears it wasn't on his order sheet. Five minutes later, they walked out with a cooler."

Pat tapped the marker against the table. "Classic drop. Eyes see a wine case in, cooler out, nobody asks questions."

"They're running these like clockwork," Jeff said.

Pat nodded. "That's their strategy. Consistency breeds invisibility. Members become accustomed to a rhythm. The same trucks, the same faces, the same motions. Eventually, they stop noticing it."

Jeff leaned back. "Which means if we move too soon..."

"We spook them," Pat finished. "And the green stays hidden."

***

Maria Torres stepped forward, carrying her own folder. She laid out several rough sketches of the women's locker room. "I spotted another unmarked camera. Facing the hallway mirror. It's not on the Club's internal list. Someone's got a separate feed."

Pat studied the drawing. "Cartel eyes. They're building redundancy. If they lose control of the Club system, they still have their own."

Kevin arrived a few minutes later, smelling faintly of fryer oil, and sat in the last chair. "Kitchen freezer's got a false wall," he said. "Thin enough to knock on and hear the hollow. I think it's storage. Temporary, not permanent."

Pat added another line on the board. "Short-term cache. They use it for holding between deliveries and vault transfers."

The agents sat in silence for a moment, examining the web of connections. Every discovery confirmed what Pat had suspected: the remodel was less about improving the Club and more about turning it into a fortress for laundering money. The hidden vaults were the holes cut into granite, invisible to casual observers.

"This isn't just a Club anymore," Pat said finally. "It's a node. Cash, stones, bonds; they flow through here like irrigation water through a canal. The board sold themselves as caretakers, but they're gatekeepers for the cartel."

Jeff exhaled. "So where's our Coffin Rock?"

Pat pointed at the board. "Everywhere. Cameras, vaults, deliveries. Obstacles in the middle of the fairway. Hit straight at them, and we lose the ball. Play the angle, though…"

"And we see the green," Maria finished.

***

That night, the Club glowed with lamplight as members dined and laughed, unaware of the secrets beneath their feet. The humidor doors gleamed, and the wine cellar was chilled. On camera, it all appeared refined. In truth, it was a graveyard of secrets.

Hole #16 required precision, not power. Pat knew the lesson well: don't fall for the temptation of the open fairway. Play wide. Be patient. Find the right line. The coffin-shaped rock in the middle of the hole wasn't meant to be conquered; it was meant to punish arrogance.

He looked once more at the board before locking up for the night.

Somewhere, beyond the cameras and the hidden walls, the path to the green was waiting.

Soon, his team would be prepared to take the shot.

Hole #17 – "Toppers Creek" 189-yard par 3

"Well, this night sure went to shit fast," Taylor Duncan said, still half-laughing, half-breathless.

Thirty minutes earlier, he'd had Stacy Broomer pressed against him on the sticky dance floor at Hung Far Low. The bass had thumped, her perfume cutting sharply through the haze of beer and fried food, and their lips were locked in a way that left little doubt about how the night would end until the bouncer tapped his shoulder.

"You two need to get a room," the man said flatly, and the pair was ushered out onto the sidewalk with the embarrassed laughter of patrons trailing behind.

Taylor didn't care. Stacy was giggling, tugging him toward his lifted F-150. He gunned the truck south through the neon haze of downtown before heading north toward her apartment in Ridgefield. She was twenty-one, finishing her last year at the university, and she had recently moved out of her childhood home, away from her parents' prying eyes and ears. What she hadn't been prepared for was how much her two roommates acted like her parents... nosey to a fault.

By the time he turned onto the dark stretch of county road leading to her neighborhood, the warmth of their earlier laughter had faded. Stacy leaned into him, her voice softer.

"Did you see the guy in the corner?" she asked.

Taylor frowned. "Which guy?"

"The one in the black jacket. He wasn't dancing. He wasn't drinking either. Just... watching."

Taylor snorted. "Stace, that's every bar in Portland. Creeps are a given."

But she shook her head. "No. This was different. He wasn't watching the crowd. He was watching *us*."

Taylor glanced in the rearview mirror out of instinct. Empty road, nothing but his own taillights bouncing off the trees. He gripped the wheel tighter.

And that's when he saw it.

At first, he thought it was a branch caught in the roadside brush, pale and awkward.

As the truck's headlights swung over the ditch, the shape became clear. Fingers.

"Jesus," Taylor muttered, braking hard. Gravel crunched as the truck skidded to the shoulder. Stacy grabbed the dash.

"What?" she asked. Then she saw it too. Her voice caught. "Oh my God, is that a hand?"

***

Pat's phone buzzed just after midnight. He had learned to recognize certain tones, specific vibrations, even before checking the screen. This one meant Bureau.

"Garrot," he answered.

"Local deputies pulled a body out of Feller's Creek," the voice on the line said. "A couple of kids spotted a hand in the ditch. The sheriff's office called it in. Thought you'd want to know."

Pat rubbed at his eyes. "Who?"

Not identified yet. Male, mid-thirties maybe. No wallet or ID. They're bringing him to the coroner now. The only thing he had on him, in the front right pocket of his jeans, was a ball marker with the Clubs logo on it.

Pat exhaled slowly. Deaths weren't uncommon: accidents, DUIs, bar fights gone too far. But the timing made his teeth grind.

The cartel had been moving this past month: deliveries tightening, pickups happening within narrower windows, paranoia simmering beneath the surface. A body in a creek was a message, whether intended or not.

***

The next morning, the Club buzzed as if nothing had happened. Members teed off at dawn, staff polished silverware, and sunlight shimmered on the stonework around the new patio. But inside, suspicion grew thick like humidity.

In the lounge, Jeff Phillips overheard two maintenance workers whispering in Spanish near the supply closet.

He caught fragments: "la policía," "el chico muerto," "cuidado." The words sharpened the edges of his stance.

Later, Maria Torres reported a new tension among the servers. The conversations' energy died when she entered. Laughter faded, replaced by side-eyes.

Kevin Dunn, working the kitchen shift, noticed a deliveryman he hadn't seen before. Broad shoulders, buzz cut, sleeves rolled up to reveal tattoos. The man didn't speak; he just wheeled in two crates of fish, parked them by the freezer, and left without a word. Kevin checked the manifest later; no fish order had been placed.

The hidden caches were filling up, and now bodies were appearing. The green at Toppers Creek was in sight, but it was perched on a narrow ledge surrounded by water. One wrong shot, and your ball would drown.

***

That afternoon, Pat summoned his "operatives" to the dungeon conference room. The board on the wall looked busier than ever, threads crossing each other until the whole thing resembled a spider's web.

"Body last night," he started without any introduction. "Thirty-eight-year-old male, preliminary ID is Pedro Delgado. He's connected to cartel operations in Tacoma.

Locally, he's been working with the grounds crew here at the Club for around six months. I guess he was either skimming or someone thought he was."

Also, Davis Pearson, Head Greenskeeper, has been a 'no-show' for the better part of a week and has not returned any calls. We sent a couple of local deputies to his home in the Highlands, and it appears to be vacant. Uncollected mail and parcels are visible on the front porch, and the house is buttoned up tight and dark.

Jeff leaned forward. "So they're cleaning house."

"Or sending a signal," Maria said.

Pat nodded. "Either way, suspicion is rising. They're watching more closely. Cameras, pickups, even their own people. We've got to assume every move is under scrutiny."

Kevin crossed his arms. "Which means we're running out of room."

Pat tapped the marker against the board. "Not out of room. Just on a par three with water in front. You don't smash the driver here. You finesse the iron. You land soft."

He pointed to the new leads: Delgado, Tacoma, body in the creek. "This is their mistake. A dead courier draws attention. Locals will ask questions.

Reporters will sniff around. That's the heat they didn't want. Which means cracks are forming."

***

By nightfall, cartel monitors had become quite restless. In a nondescript warehouse two counties away, three men gathered around screens showing mirrored Club feeds. One rewound the morning footage from the kitchen, watching Kevin walk past the crates of fish.

"Ese no es cocinero normal," the man muttered. "He looks too careful."

Another zoomed in on Maria serving drinks in the lounge, her smile professional, but her eyes constantly scanning.

"Y ella", he said. "Too aware. Not like the others."

The third man, who had been silent until now, finally spoke. "If there are eyes inside the Club, we'll know soon. Keep watching. The rock always shows who's strong enough to carry it and who falls short."

***

Back at the Club, Pat strolled the grounds at dusk. Hole #17 stretched ahead, with Toppers Creek crossing in front of the green. A golfer needed accuracy here, not strength. Too short, and the ball sank into the water. Too long, and it rolled into the rough behind. The green sat like a challenge.

He thought of Delgado's body, the hand reaching out of the ditch like a warning. Someone had misjudged the distance. Someone had fallen short.

And now, suspicion floated like mist over the creek.

Pat exhaled, aware that the game was accelerating. The upcoming shots would demand perfection. One mistake, and everything would fall into the water below.

Hole #18 – "Devil's Backbone" 453-yard par 4

The eighteenth hole at the Club was well-known among its members. A long par four, with a fairway that rose like a ridge and was as narrow as a ribbon. Locals called it the Devil's Backbone. Shots that drifted even a few yards left or right would bounce down steep slopes into the rough, leaving golfers to hack their way back uphill. Shoot it straight, and the green was within reach. Miss, and the hole would swallow you.

Pat thought about that ridge while sitting in the dungeon conference room, marker in hand. His soldiers sat around the table, their faces tighter than usual. The cartel's suspicion was no longer just a theory; it was real, alive, and pressing in.

Jeff was the first to notice it. Two nights ago, a member named Barrow cornered him in the lounge; too smooth, too inquisitive. He asked Jeff where he grew up, what school he attended, and why someone his age wasn't in college. The questions seemed casual, but his tone suggested importance. Jeff dodged the questions, but the encounter cast a shadow.

Maria's report was worse. She came into the locker room that morning to find her purse moved and her notepad open on the counter. Nothing was taken, but the message was clear: we can touch your things, we can touch you, whenever we want.

Kevin saw two men at the loading dock, both strangers, both watching him unload deliveries. They didn't speak, just stared until he left.

The cartel wasn't just guessing anymore. They were actively probing.

Pat set the marker down and folded his hands. "We're walking the Backbone now. One wrong step, and we slide into the ravine."

***

The Bureau quietly strengthened its team. Pat hadn't informed them yet, but two of the newer "hires" weren't just FBI assets; they were DEA agents.

The first was Allison Kane, hired last week as a bartender. Blonde hair tied back in a simple ponytail, eyes like flint. She poured drinks with a smile, but her real skill was surveillance; she could memorize an entire room in minutes.

Allison had spent three years embedded in cartel operations in Arizona before being rotated out.

The second was Marcus Lee, a line cook in the kitchen. He looked constantly busy, apron stained with bacon grease and flour, a man who went unnoticed. But Marcus had learned his skills tracking narcotics shipments from Mexico through Texas. His specialty was following the money trails hidden inside legitimate businesses.

Together, they weren't just reinforcements; they were a lifeline.

Pat finally revealed the truth that night. "Kane and Lee are DEA. They've been working with us from the beginning.

That was part of Henry's plan. If one agency fell, the other would still be active. We're not alone."

Jeff blinked in surprise. Maria leaned back in her chair, eyebrows raised. Kevin let out a low whistle.

"You kept that quiet," he said.

Pat allowed himself a slight grin. "That's the point of a hidden green. You don't see it until you need to."

***

Outside the Club, cartel suspicion turned to action.

In a warehouse illuminated by flickering fluorescent lights, Jon José leaned over a bank of monitors. Footage of the club scrolled across the screens: kitchens, hallways, locker rooms, loading docks. His lieutenants flanked him, one smoking, the other jotting down notes.

"Too many new faces," José said. "The busboy. The bartender. The cook. They think we don't notice? We notice everything."

The man with the cigarette exhaled smoke toward the ceiling. "You want them tested?"

José nodded. "Yes. Push them. See if they crack. Anyone who does-" He mimed pulling a trigger.

The lieutenants nodded. The test would come soon.

***

It arrived two days later, subtle at first.

Maria was called into a private dining room to serve a group of board members and their guests. Halfway through pouring wine, one of the men, a contractor with a too-wide grin, asked her to fetch a specific bottle from the cellar. Not just any bottle, but one stored on the pivoting rack.

Her pulse spiked. The request was deliberate, a trap. If she didn't understand the mechanism, she'd stumble. If she did, she'd reveal herself.

She smiled politely, nodded, and left the room. In the hallway, she pulled out her phone and texted Allison Kane: *Cellar test. Help.*

Allison arrived five minutes later, carrying a tray of glassware. She entered the cellar with Maria, her voice steady. "I'll distract them. You grab a different vintage. Something close. Blame inventory."

Maria followed the instructions, choosing a similar bottle and going back to the table. The men grumbled, but she apologized smoothly, blaming stock rotation. They overlooked it for now.

Back in the cellar, Allison leaned against the cool stone wall. "That was their shot across the bow. Next one will be sharper."

***

Meanwhile, Jeff faced his own challenge. One of the maintenance workers, a stocky man with a shaved head, approached him in the staff lot. He threw Jeff a set of keys.

"Drive this to Tacoma," he said, pointing to a van parked by the fence. "No questions, no stops. Drop it at the address in the glovebox."

Jeff forced a grin. "I just started, man. Shouldn't someone else... "

The man's gaze hardened. "No. You."

Jeff felt the trap closing in. If he refused, suspicion would rise. If he drove the van, he'd be trafficking for the cartel. He needed a third option.

He accepted the keys with a nod, then stepped away briefly to text Pat. Minutes later, Marcus Lee arrived at his side, wiping his hands on his apron.

"I'll follow the kid, and we can drive back together," Marcus said casually, as if it were the most natural thing in the world. "Make sure the rookie doesn't get lost. And we both get paid for a relaxed drive to Tacoma and back."

Together, they drove. Halfway to Tacoma, Marcus found a rest stop, said he needed a smoke, and while Jeff kept watch, he slipped a tracker into the van's wheel well.

They delivered the van, handed over the keys, and left silently.

Later, back at the club, Marcus whispered to Pat, "That van's going to lead us to their distribution node. They thought they were testing Jeff. Instead, they gave us a free trial."

***

Pat studied the web on his board that night, threads connected tighter than ever, lines converging on nodes that pulsed with significance. The cartel's suspicion had sped up the timeline, but it had also opened doors.

The DEA's presence strengthened his position. The cartel's challenges had made his people demonstrate their resilience under pressure. The green was still concealed, but he could now perceive its outline.

The Devil's Backbone was unforgiving. One misstep, and the entire team could fall. But if they kept their shots steady and trusted positioning over power, they could crest the ridge and see everything.

Pat capped his marker and leaned back, exhaling.

Soon, everything would work in their favor, or it would go terribly wrong. What did they say in the military, "FUBAR."

The 19th Hole – Clubhouse

The storm broke just after sundown.

Members lingered in the dining room, wineglasses chiming, laughter spilling into the halls. On the surface, it was just another successful night at the club. But behind the walls, the game had reached its final hole. Every player knew it, whether they admitted it or not.

Pat Garrot sat in his office, the glow of his monitor casting a pale light across the room. No one was watching the comings and goings inside. It was near an outside entrance, and that door was labeled 'Fire Sprinkler Control Room.'

The Cartel hadn't considered this area anything more than what it was signed for: a utility room used by firefighters during their annual inspection of the Club's sprinkler system.

His board stood in the corner, threads converging like arteries into the heart of the Club.

Every line pointed here, tonight. The cartel's suspicion had turned to certainty. His team had been tested, prodded, and finally marked. There would be no more delays.

The radio in his desk drawer crackled. Marcus Lee's voice: "They're staging. Two vans are in the south lot. Armed. I count six men."

Maria approached next, her voice strained. "Board members are gathering in the private lounge. Not for cocktails. This feels wrong."

Then Jeff said, "Security feeds just went dark. Someone's cut the loop."

Pat's stomach dropped. The match was over. The final strokes were already underway.

"Stay sharp," he said into the radio. "This is the hole that matters. Eyes up, positions steady. Remember, don't try to win it all in one swing. Play position."

***

The first shots shattered glass.

A volley from the south entrance, with two cartel enforcers blowing out the door and storming into the hallway. Members screamed, ducking under tables. Staff scattered.

Jeff was near the bar, clearing dishes, when the gunfire started. He ducked behind the counter, drew the Kimber from his ankle holster, and returned fire. One of the intruders fell, the other spun away wounded.

Maria was already moving, guiding panicked guests toward the rear exit. She drew her own weapon, covering the retreat, her calm voice cutting through the chaos: "Stay low, keep moving, eyes forward."

In the kitchen, Marcus turned off the lights and pulled Kevin into cover. Two more gunmen burst through the loading dock, guns aimed. Marcus fired first, the shot ringing out in the steel room, hitting one. Kevin, heart pounding, finished off the second.

Allison Kane's voice cut through the comms. "East wing, two more inbound. Board members are arming themselves. Whitcomb's among them."

Pat left his office, Glock in hand, rushing down the main hall. He could already smell smoke, sharp and bitter. Around the corner, he saw the Board president, Hal Whitcomb, standing with Jon José and two lieutenants. They were armed, eyes wild but calculating.

"You think you can burn this place down, Garrot?" Whitcomb sneered. "You think your strings and charts make you smarter than us? This Club is ours."

Pat leveled his weapon. "Not anymore."

**

Gunfire erupted again, turning the hall into chaos: shouts, ricochets, and plaster dust falling from the ceiling. Pat fired and hit one of the lieutenants in the shoulder. Allison flanked from the east corridor, her shots precise, dropping the second.

José ducked behind a pillar and fired wild bursts. Whitcomb dove into a side room, dragging a satchel. Pat moved forward carefully, motioning Allison to follow.

In the lounge, Jeff and Maria had herded the last of the guests out the back. Once the civilians were gone, they rejoined the fight, sweeping through the hallways room by room. Marcus and Kevin came along, smoke still clinging to their clothes.

The team gathered in the main lounge where Whitcomb had taken cover. The satchel was open on the table, filled with stacks of cash, sparkling stones, and documents stamped with foreign seals; enough evidence to ruin dozens of careers.

Whitcomb raised his weapon, sweat pouring down his face. "You don't know who you're dealing with. We have gone far beyond this place. Kill me, and a hundred more will take my place."

Pat held his ground, eyes fixed on him. "Maybe. But tonight, it's over."

Whitcomb's finger twitched on the trigger. Maria fired first. The shot hit him in the chest. He collapsed against the table, eyes wide, the satchel spilling onto the floor.

Jon José dashed for the back door, desperation overtaking his bravado. He didn't get far. Marcus's gunshot rang out, and José collapsed at the threshold.

Silence settled, interrupted only by the crackle of flames from a burning curtain.

***

The aftermath unfolded quickly. Sirens blared outside, red and blue lights flooding the shattered clubhouse windows. FBI, DEA, and local law enforcement arrived. The cavalry was too late for the fight but on time for the cleanup.

Agents flooded in, securing bodies, grabbing the satchel, and pulling hard drives from everything with a hard drive, including the cartel's mirrored camera feeds. Members huddled outside under blankets, shaken but alive.

Pat stood on the front steps, watching Whitcomb's body being loaded into a van. Smoke curled from the roof, but the fire was under control.

His team gathered around him, bruised, exhausted, but still standing.

"You played it straight," Pat told them softly. "Devil's Backbone. Narrow ridge. You stayed on it. That's why we're still standing."

Jeff managed a tired grin. Maria exhaled deeply, finally relaxing her shoulders. Marcus lit a cigarette, his hands trembling slightly. Allison simply nodded, her eyes already scanning the perimeter for threats that might not even come.

This match was over.

***

Hours later, with the Club cordoned off and evidence trucks arriving, Pat sat alone in his office one last time.

The board still stood in the corner, with threads leading everywhere. However, the center had now collapsed. Whitcomb gone. José gone. The laundering is exposed.

He took out a new folder from his drawer, labeled in black ink: After Action.

He began to write.

The operation ended with a confrontation at the clubhouse.

Casualties included four cartel enforcers, two lieutenants, Board President Whitcomb, and Cartel Lieutenant Jon José.

Seized assets consist of $22.3 million in cash, gems, and negotiable bonds. Surveillance feeds have been secured. There were no civilian casualties. Mission accomplished.

Pat paused, pen hanging in the air. Success, yes. But he knew better than to believe the game was over. Whitcomb had been right about one thing: power didn't pass with a single man.

The course had more holes. The match was over, but the tournament continued.

He capped the pen, closed the file, and leaned back in his chair, staring at the first pink streaks of dawn.

Tomorrow, he would brief Henry Wellborne. Tomorrow, the Bureau would include this chapter in its records.

But tonight, for a brief moment, Pat let himself feel the weight lift. The Devil's Backbone had been crossed.

And for now, that was sufficient.

Chapter Twenty – After Action Report

In Washington, D.C., the morning air had a damp chill, the kind that seeped into the bones. Much like the other Washington, he had just left. Pat pulled his coat tighter as he fell into step beside Henry Wellborne. The two men moved slowly along the gravel paths winding through the Smithsonian complex, the pale marble facades glowing in the morning sun.

Henry suggested the location, calling it neutral ground. In D.C., that meant a place where power whispered through history but didn't stay long enough to be eavesdropped on.

"You look tired," Henry said after a stretch of silence.

Pat gave a humorless laugh. "That's because I am. A week of paperwork after a night of gunfire will do that."

Henry nodded, eyes drifting toward the Washington Monument in the distance. "But you kept your team alive. And you pulled Whitcomb and the others off the board. That's no small thing."

Pat didn't answer immediately. He watched a group of schoolchildren march by, chattering and bouncing their backpacks. He thought of the Club members huddled in blankets outside the smoking building, faces pale but still alive. Success is measured in survivors.

"We hit the green," Pat finally said. "But the course isn't finished. You know that as well as I do."

Henry's mouth curved into a thin smile. "Let's walk through it. Take me through your holes from start to finish. Consider this your official after-action interview."

***

Pat inhaled slowly, as if pulling the story up from his boots.

"They started small," he said. "Bylaws changed, contracts flowing. Cart paths, clubhouse redesign, all camouflage for the laundering. Whitcomb as the face, José as the architect. They turned that Club into a node, a transfer hub. Cash, bonds, stones. Hidden vaults in the wine cellar and humidor. Cartel couriers disguised as maintenance and delivery men. Drops and pickups choreographed to look routine."

Henry nodded, hands clasped behind his back. "And the cameras?"

"Everywhere," Pat said. "Club feeds mirrored to cartel monitors. They thought they were untouchable. Our people were blind until we started planting our own lenses. The game turned into layers of surveillance; ours over theirs, theirs over ours. Like chess on two boards stacked on top of each other."

Henry grunted. "And suspicion?"

It grew quickly. They encountered many new faces: Jeff, Maria, Kevin, then Allison and Marcus. They tested them, cornered them, and tried to flush them out. Almost succeeded, too. The wine cellar incident with Maria and the van with Jeff were close calls. But our people held their ground.

The DEA cover was the safety net, and Kane and Lee gave us the advantage.

They turned a corner, with the Air and Space Museum shining to their right. Pat squinted against the sun.

"Delgado's body in Toppers Creek was the turning point," he said. "That was their Coffin Rock. A misstep. It revealed that paranoia had broken their own system. They were killing couriers and sending signals. That confirmed it: the endgame was near."

Henry paused to watch a flock of pigeons scatter from the path. "And the confrontation?"

Pat's jaw tightened. "They came in armed. Two vans, south lot. Gunfire through the clubhouse doors.

Guests panicked, staff scattered. We'd prepared for surveillance, not open combat, but the team adapted. Jeff is at the bar. Marcus and Kevin are in the kitchen. Maria is clearing civilians. Allison is flanking the hall. I faced Whitcomb and José directly. It ended with both dead. Satchel recovered cash, gems, and documents."

Henry was quiet for a long moment. Then: "Casualties?"

Cartel side: eight, including both leaders. Ours: none. Civilian: none.

Henry's lips pressed into a thin line of satisfaction. "That's clean. Cleaner than I expected."

Pat shrugged. "Luck, discipline, and a little bit of timing. But it won't stay clean. Whitcomb was right, they've got reach. You cut off one head, another grows."

***

They passed the Castle, its red sandstone walls glowing in the morning light. Henry slowed down, resting one hand briefly on the low iron fence.

"You've carried a heavy load," he said. "You turned a golf club into a battlefield and walked your team off the course alive. The Bureau will call this a success, and it is one. But you're right, the match isn't over. Just one round finished."

Pat felt the weight behind Henry's words. Success always seemed temporary, passing. Like hitting a good shot on the 18th, you could enjoy it for a moment before recalling the next round was waiting.

Henry faced him again, eyes intense. "There's another one."

Pat's stomach tightened. "Another Club?"

Henry nodded. "Different city, different disguise. This one's not about golf. It's a private equity Club. Marinas instead of fairways. Same cartel fingerprints. Same blueprint. And now they'll be even more cautious because of what you did in Washington."

Pat exhaled, watching a jogger glide past. "So you want me to tee it up again."

Henry smiled faintly. "You've already got the swing for it. We'll brief you fully soon. For now, file your reports and get some rest. But don't get too comfortable."

***

They walked in silence for a while, gravel crunching underfoot, the hum of traffic faint at the edges of the mall. Finally, Pat spoke.

"You ever think about how golf mirrors this work?" he asked.

Henry raised an eyebrow. "Go on."

Every hole is different, but the fundamentals stay the same. You line up, swing, and read the terrain. Sometimes the green is hidden; sometimes the fairway narrows to nothing; sometimes there's a rock right in the middle. Still, you keep playing because the match isn't just about one hole; it's about the whole course.

Henry chuckled softly. "Poetic, for a man with chalkboards full of string."

Pat smiled for the first time that morning. "Even game theory has room for metaphor."

They paused at the steps of the Natural History Museum. Henry reached out his hand. Pat shook it firmly.

"Good work," Henry said. "Now get ready for the next match."

Pat nodded, already sensing the course ahead, with hidden dangers waiting. The first round had ended. The next was already approaching.

Chapter Twenty-One – Offshore Shenanigans

The Gulf shimmered like hammered silver beneath the late afternoon sun. Pat Garrot stood at the edge of a marina in the Florida Panhandle, the air thick with the scent of salt and diesel as pelicans circled and dove lazily near the docks. He had flown down from Washington that morning, Henry's words still echoing in his mind: There's another one.

This wasn't a golf region, even though there were courses. Instead, it was a boating area; yachts, fishing boats, sailboats with colorful hulls. Wealth floated here, gently bobbing in slips, and Pat could already sense the same currents that had moved beneath the fairways of the Club.

A tall man in aviator sunglasses stepped out from the shadow of the yacht club's colonnade. He was dressed casually in a linen shirt and khakis but carried himself with the stillness of someone trained to notice details.

"Agent Garrot," he said, extending his hand. "Or should I say Mr. Johnson, prospective member of Bay Haven Yacht Club."

Pat shook the hand firmly. "Either works."

The man gave a slight smile. "Special Agent Colin Mercer, DEA. Welcome to Florida."

They fell into step, walking along the dockside path. Mercer nodded toward the main building: two stories of cream stucco, glass windows sparkling in the sun, a flag fluttering from the roof. "Bay Haven looks like a playground for retirees and Gulf Coast money." Below, it's the same game you've been playing in Washington. Different type of course, same hazards.

Pat listened, eyes scanning the rows of boats: fifty-footers with polished decks, racing yachts with sails furled tight, sportfishing rigs bristling with rods and antennas. Every vessel represented wealth, and wealth, Pat knew, was a perfect tool for laundering.

Mercer continued. "Here, it's not hidden vaults or wine cellars. It's hull compartments, shipping manifests, and shell ownership. Millions can move in cash or stones from one marina to another under the guise of maintenance or fishing charters. Add in offshore accounts, and it's clean as a whistle by the time it hits the banks."

They paused at a slip where a yacht named Emerald Dawn rocked gently. Its flag displayed the crest of Bay Haven Yacht Club, with stylized sails intertwined over a compass rose.

"This one?" Pat asked.

Mercer nodded. "Owned by a shell company in Belize. Payments were wired from Panama. Last month, the Coast Guard spotted it 30 miles offshore, rendezvousing with a freighter registered in Venezuela.

Nothing was seized; they were too cautious, but we understand what it signifies. And two of Bay Haven's board members were aboard."

Pat felt the knot of recognition tighten in his gut. Same structure, same arrogance. The Board wasn't a board; it was a gatekeeper for cartel money. The golf club had been a green fairway with hidden traps. The yacht club was open water, deep and shifting, where the hazards could swallow whole ships.

"Who's running point?" Pat asked.

Mercer slipped off his sunglasses, revealing eyes rimmed with fatigue. "Name's Victor Castellano. Cuban-American, mid-fifties, came up through shipping out of Miami. Charismatic, smart, ruthless.

Loves rubies, same as José did. Runs Bay Haven as if it were his personal kingdom. And if you thought Whitcomb had friends in high places, Castellano has senators on speed dial."

Pat examined the yacht, its white hull shining. "And you want me to play member."

Mercer smiled. "You already know the drill. New face, credible cover, time spent at the bar and the boardroom. Only this time, you'll be dealing with the ocean instead of the fairway."

***

That evening, Pat sat alone on the balcony of a rented condo overlooking the Gulf.

Below, the surf whispered against the shore, and the horizon was painted orange by the sinking sun. He opened his notebook, the same one he'd used in Washington, and wrote at the top of a new page:

Bay Haven Yacht Club – Florida Panhandle

He listed the names Mercer had given him: Castellano, two board members, and three contractors connected to boat maintenance. He drew the first rough web, lines radiating like rigging from a mast.

He could almost hear Henry's voice: every hole has its own hazards. Learn the terrain before you swing.

Pat leaned back in his chair, listening to the sea. In Washington, the Club had been a place of hidden greens and coffin rocks. Here, it would be reefs and tides, vessels and manifests. But the structure of the game hadn't changed.

There were still players, strategies, payoffs, and equilibrium. And there would be suspicion, betrayal, and eventually, confrontation.

He closed the notebook, exhaling through his nose. The match in Washington was over, but here in Florida, the first round was still ahead.

Pat stood, watching the last light fade across the water, and felt the familiar weight settle back onto his shoulders. The game wasn't over. It never was.

Tomorrow, the Bay Haven Yacht Club will welcome a new member, and the regatta will begin.

Epilogue

The fairways of Washington have been conquered, but the waters of the Gulf run deeper, darker, and far less forgiving. At Bay Haven Yacht Club, fortunes are hidden in polished hulls and offshore ledgers, and the stakes rise with every tide. Pat Garrot has walked the course; now he must sail into a new game, where every wave conceals a trap, and every handshake hides a dagger.

The game isn't finished. It has just shifted to open water.